THE EX 1%ERS

TROY KOERNTJES

FOREWORDS TONY "JACK THE BEAR" MANTZ AND DENNIS ESPIRITU

TABLE OF CONTENTS

BY TONY "JACK THE BEAR" MANTZ

Now, before you think this book is another typical true crime book full of the usual stereotypes, I'm here to tell you this one is different. Sure, the backdrop evolves around the inner workings of life being a 1% er in an outlaw motorcycle club, but that's not the real story here.

This is a book about redemption. A true story about my friend Troy, who managed to pull off what many have attempted, but fell short and often with dire consequences. He successfully left a club in good standing, which in and of itself is quite remarkable. But if that wasn't enough, he also transformed his own life, while inspiring others to do the same. This puts him in an entirely different echelon.

Sure, you'll get some insights about life in an outlaw motorcycle club with all the gory details, but this does not glorify the life. If anything, it's a cautionary tale told with great honesty and transparency. How a man overcame his demons, going into detail that will give you a new appreciation of how debilitating mental illness can be (if you've been lucky enough not to experience it).

This book gives hope. It proves that no matter how bleak your life may be, there always is a way out and not only that, but that you can make the most extraordinary U-turn you wouldn't think possible.

I invite you to read this book, discarding any bias or preconceived notions you have. You will come to the end of this restoring your faith in The Human Spirit, feeling more empathy for the growing number of men in this country dealing with their own private hell.

I'm proud of my brother Troy for bringing these voices together. Proud that he's turned his own journey into a platform for change. And proud that he's giving the next generation a chance to learn from those who've been there, done it, and walked away with lessons worth sharing.

So read with an open mind. Read with compassion. And let these stories remind you that no matter what patch you wear — or wore — healing and growth are possible.

Respect,
Tony "Jack the Bear" Mantz

BY DENNIS ESPIRITU

My name is Dennis Espiritu. I'm Filipino, born to immigrant parents, and I grew up in Melbourne's South East—in the Dandenong and Springvale areas. My parents worked hard, gave me every chance to succeed, but I threw it all away. By the 1990s, I was caught in the grip of the heroin epidemic. What started as trying to escape life turned into twenty-five years of crime, chaos, and destruction. Heroin owned me. It stole my freedom, my identity, and every ounce of self-respect I had.

By 38, I was done. Broken. Another junkie statistic if I didn't change. Rehab became the turning point—the place I finally faced myself and started rebuilding.

And once I got out, life lined me up with two men who would change everything: Troy Koerntjes from Complete Health Geelong and Jacob Little from About Time for Justice.

These weren't your average blokes. Both were ex–club members. Both carried the weight of that life. And yet, like me, they'd made the decision to rebuild instead of rot. When we met, it was instant. No bullshit. No judgement. Just three men who had been through hell and knew exactly what it felt like.

"Beyond the Backpatch" is more than a story to me; it's a journey that hits close to home. It's about life after the club, stepping away from everything you've known, and facing the world without the structure, identity, and brotherhood that once defined you. It's about the struggle, the freedom, and the unexpected opportunities that come when you leave the only life you've ever known.

At RUN THAT REHAB, I feel strongly about contributing to this book because stories like this matter—especially for men like me. Vulnerability is often seen as weakness, and as men, we're expected to be tough, to hide our struggles. But being open about mental health, mistakes, and growth? That's where real strength comes from.

I've personally witnessed Troy turn his life around, moving from a past that could have kept him trapped in the same destructive patterns to a life of purpose and impact. His story is inspiring and shows what's possible when you face your past head-on and choose to create a better future. By contributing to this book, I want to show that there's power in honesty, courage in growth, and hope beyond the backpatch.

What's kept us solid isn't just the wins—it's the struggles. We found strength *inside* the struggle, and we found even more strength in vulnerability. Most men think vulnerability is weakness. But when you've lived what we've lived, you know it's the opposite. Vulnerability builds trust. It closes the gap. It makes the bond unbreakable. Because when you can drop the mask and say, *"I'm struggling,"* and your brothers don't flinch—that's when you know you've got something real. That's when you know you can lean on each other when the weight gets heavy.

Since then, we've spoken at seminars, fronted events, jumped on podcasts, sat across from investors, and hosted networking dinners where people don't just eat—they leave with connections. Podcasters, influencers, singers, boxers—you name it. Everyone walks out with value, and everyone benefits. That's the standard we set.

And here's the truth—between the three of us, our network is insane. Mental health. Addiction recovery. Institutional abuse. The doors we've opened, the people we've connected with, the opportunities we've created—it's massive. And the bond runs so deep that when one of us is mentioned, the other two are in the same sentence.

That's also where Run That Rehab comes in. It's my personal platform—therapy for the streets. I break content down into bite-sized pieces—raw, simple, easy to digest. Because I know the viewer who is still in active addiction might not have the focus for a book or a lecture. But if they can watch just *one* reel a day, every reel contains a nugget. And by the time they're ready to change, they'll look at the Run That Rehab platform and find a gold mine—insight, mindset, perspective—all there for them to leverage and guide their recovery. You can find me at @RunThatRehab on Facebook, Instagram, TikTok, Snapchat, and YouTube.

Every Monday night, I bring that energy into the brotherhood I share with Troy and Jacob. Together, we go live on TikTok. No scripts, no polished speeches—just raw truth. We answer questions, share our stories, and give people solutions they can actually use. Three different voices, one mission: giving back.

Run That Rehab started with a mission to lift this city off its knees. But as times change, so *has* the narrative. Now, it's time to raise the nation.

For me, it's simple: Troy and Jacob didn't walk into my life when I was still broken. They came in once I'd made the choice to rebuild—and together, we've been building ever since. They're not just mates. They're brothers. And with Run That Rehab, I bring my part to the table—complementing what we're creating together and proving to anyone watching: no matter how far you've fallen, there's always a way back.

RUN THAT REHAB. Run your life. Or it'll run you.

Dennis Espirtu

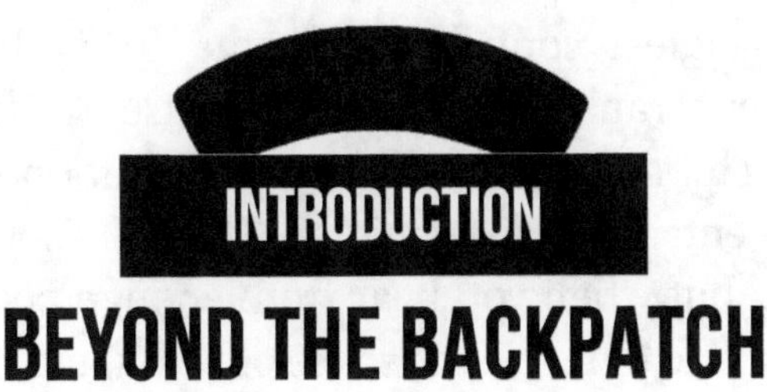

BEYOND THE BACKPATCH

In these pages, you'll read stories from real ex-1%ers — their reasons, their thoughts, their experiences. Not in a self-serving, reputation-boosting way, but with honesty: the good and the bad.

Most of the people you'll meet in this book are now community leaders in fields like mental health, alcohol, and drug services. Some are still finding their feet after leaving club life. I myself am now a qualified counsellor, running a mental health and disability service and charity. None of us are telling these stories to impress. We're telling them because the truth matters.

The men and women sharing their stories here have been through the thick of it. Some came out the other side stronger; others were not so lucky. All of them paid a price. By opening up about their pasts, they're offering something rare: an unfiltered look at the realities of life inside a motorcycle club, and the toll it can take long after the patch is gone.

Our goal is simple: to give you a real picture, so you can make an informed decision about whether "club life" is for you — or whether the cost is too high. These stories aren't about glorifying gang life. They're about stripping away the myths and letting you see what really happens behind closed doors, on the runs, in the meetings, and in the quiet moments when the adrenaline wears off.

To cover all angles, contributors come from different clubs, holding different ranks and roles. Because while clubs share similarities, each one runs by its own constitution — often strict, sometimes eccentric, always unique. There is no single "truth" about club life, but when you hear from enough people who lived it, patterns begin to emerge: the sense of belonging, the hunger for respect, the battles for power, and the loneliness that often lies beneath it all.

Over the coming chapters, you'll learn the basics too. When someone mentions a "prospect," a "nom," or a "run," you'll know what they mean. You'll see how the theory of "Family, Work, Club" is supposed to guide priorities — and how, in practice, club life often takes over everything. Members are expected to give time, money, and loyalty without question. Full members face compulsory events: at least one day a week plus two events a month, with attendance not just expected but demanded. Prospects and noms take on even more: cleaning shifts, extra nights, last-minute meetings, and whatever else is thrown their way.

None of this is written to warn or to encourage. It's written to inform. Club life isn't just leather, patches, and brotherhood. It's politics, pressure, sacrifices, and consequences.

This book isn't here to glorify the patch. It's here to go beyond it — to show what lies underneath. The lives, the trauma, the choices, and the consequences. Beyond the backpatch, you'll find the truth.

OUT OF NECESSITY

The first bike clubs were born out of necessity. You could almost say they were like the Men's Sheds of today, except their point of interest was motorbikes, brotherhood, and freedom.

These clubs offered support and protection to men who felt abandoned by the world. They became safe havens where people with shared experiences could gather and be understood. And isn't that what we all crave as humans?

I remember on many occasions we used to say, *"the only ones that love us are us."* And we meant it. For many of us, the first time stepping into the clubhouse was also the first time we felt fully accepted and part of something bigger than ourselves.

Inside a motorcycle club, the order of priorities was meant to be followed: Family, Work, Club. I use the term *serving* because the origins of motorcycle clubs lay with veterans coming home from war. They returned to little or no support, and in many cases were even hated - branded "baby killers" instead of the heroes they actually were.

With no government support and hostility from the public, these men only had each other. The brotherhood they had known in wartime was all they could cling to. Imagine returning from serving your country, justly or unjustly, after enduring hell, only to be discarded, ridiculed, and shamed. Left to deal with the atrocities of war, with mental illness and disabilities... all alone.

Here, you had groups of men with fractured identities, searching for something to anchor their morals and beliefs. Their old systems had been shot down in the war. In that search for meaning arose the term *outlaw*. It filled the void, reflecting how the country itself made them feel — like outsiders and outcasts.

At the same time, culture and media turned bikers into icons. James Dean looked cool in *Rebel Without a Cause* (1955). *Easy Rider* (1969), starring Jack Nicholson, Peter Fonda, and Dennis Hopper, was hailed as "a landmark counterculture film" and "a touchstone for a generation" that "captured the national imagination." Steve McQueen made history with his famous Triumph jump in *The Great Escape* (1963). And *The Wild One* (1953), with Marlon Brando, cemented the rebellious biker image.

More modern examples followed: *Harley Davidson and the Marlboro Man* (1991), featuring Mickey Rourke, Don Johnson, and Daniel Baldwin; the cartoon *Biker Mice from Mars* (1993); *Wild Hogs* (2007), with John Travolta and Ray Liotta; and of course *Terminator 2* (1991), where Arnold Schwarzenegger — in leather jacket, shotgun in hand — rode a Fat Boy off bridges in pursuit of John Connor. (The other lead, Robert Patrick, was in fact a real-life member of one of the world's oldest motorcycle clubs.)

Today, stars like Jason Momoa are in motorcycle clubs. Ewan McGregor and Charley Boorman ride the world in their documentaries, and Keanu Reeves admits he can't go a single day without being on a bike. Newer films like *The Bikeriders* (2024), based on the true story of two of the oldest clubs, continue the tradition.

Motorcycles have long been shorthand for rebellion and freedom. They give us a romanticised glimpse behind the veil, promising escape from the grind of the 9-to-5. Add to that the lure of adventure and the ever-present "bad boy" image — not to mention the glamour of the women in these stories — and the appeal is obvious.

Even outside biker movies, bikes signal cool. In *The Karate Kid* (1984), the Cobra Kai rode dirt bikes to chase Daniel down. In *The Lost Boys* (1987), vampires terrorise the town on bikes while dressed like glam rockers, set apart from the "normal" world. Even *Happy Days* gave us Fonzie, the friendly neighbourhood biker on his Triumph.

More recently, high-quality series like *Sons of Anarchy* and its spin-offs have portrayed bikers as charismatic gangster-heroes with money, power, and women. It's no surprise club culture has surged in popularity.

During the early years, clubs didn't wear the 1% patch you see today. That came after a violent altercation between clubs drew national attention. The press turned to the American Motorcyclist Association (AMA), the country's oldest riders' rights group, to explain. In its now-famous statement, the AMA declared:

> "99% of bikers are law-abiding citizens. It's only that last one per cent who are outlaws."
> *(The Austin Chronicle)*

That one sentence gave birth to the "1%er" identity. The diamond patch, exclusive to 1% clubs, became a badge of honour. Alongside it came the three-piece back patch, which is still jealously guarded.

The three-piece consists of two *rockers* — one at the top (the club name) and one at the bottom (usually country or territory) — plus a square patch on the side that reads *MC* (Motorcycle Club). Some clubs once used the term " *MG* (Motorcycle Gang), but later switched in an attempt to improve their public image. In truth, the dictionary definition of *club* fits best:

> "An organisation of people with a common purpose or interest, who meet regularly and take part in shared activities."
> *(Cambridge Dictionary)*

Some clubs even attempted to register themselves as religions — not such a far-fetched idea when you consider the level of belief and devotion involved.

The side rocker on the front vest can mean different things in different clubs — rank, location, or even nicknames in social clubs. (Though 1% clubs don't hand out nicknames casually.) There are also *earned patches*, awarded for specific deeds. Like in Scouts, you don't get them unless you've put in the work. What's required to earn them is club business, and best left undiscussed here.

Different types of clubs wear different patches:

- **Feeder clubs:** Three-piece patches without the 1% diamond. They're usually under the protection of a larger club and act as a "try before you buy."

- **CMC/MMC clubs**: Christian Motorcycle Clubs or Military Motorcycle Clubs, with their own variations.

- **Social Motorcycle Clubs (SMCs)**: Often limited to front patches, though some now wear one-piece backs (with permission).

Even police, fire, and emergency services have clubs — the Blue, Red, and Orange Knights. Mental health workers formed the

Green Knights. In fact, these groups once met in a castle and cheekily dubbed themselves the *Knights of the Round Table.*

Most clubs also maintain *street crews.* These are people who don't ride or aren't trusted to wear colours. They handle event setup, transport, or odd jobs too risky for patched members. They're often looked down on, but they play their part.

Patches remain a source of tension. Why should grown men dictate what other men can wear? Tradition? Culture? In the biker world, the answer is yes. Like surfing's unwritten rules about catching waves, you either learn and respect them — or you pay the price.

And patches are earned. Just as it takes years to become a doctor, or a decade to earn a black belt in martial arts, it can take seven years to earn a patch. If someone just makes one up and wears it, it disrespects the years of blood, sweat, and loyalty others put in. That's why wannabes with fake online patches are such a problem. They get caught doing something stupid, and the whole club takes the blame. Some clubs even copyright their patches and sue imitators.

But don't mistake 1%ers as heartless. They show respect to veterans and community clubs. My own group, The Mental Health Militia and Complete Health Geelong, have always received nothing but positive recognition from 1% clubs.

This debate will never end. Governments have tried banning back patches, but that only inspires new clubs to spring up, as happened in the Netherlands. Outlaws don't vanish because of a ban.

And here's the truth: if you're chasing patches just for the look, club life isn't for you. It's not about fabric and thread — it's about brotherhood, sacrifice, and loyalty. Without those, you won't last.

HE AIN'T HEAVY, HE'S MY BROTHER

One thing I've never seen talked about much is a club funeral. For me — and many others — it's an incredible experience. Strange thing to say about a funeral, I know, but when you first join a club, you're told: *"You've never seen a funeral until you've seen a club funeral."* They're right. It's about honour and respect.

Members from every chapter must attend. Often, brothers fly in from overseas, along with others from the wider motorcycle community. In the days leading up to it, prospects and *noms* are busy running people to and from airports. Clubhouses are buzzing, with hosting chapters arranging accommodation, bikes, and support for visiting brothers.

The late member is taken on one last ride on a modified Harley. The coffin is carried on the shoulders of his brothers, passed down a line that can stretch hundreds deep. If the gravesite is far, once you've shouldered him, you sprint to the front to help pass him along again — never on a stretcher, because *"he ain't heavy, he's my brother."*

At the grave, after lowering the casket, every brother takes a turn with the shovel — because *"we bury our own."* Afterwards, it's a huge party of remembrance. No one is judged for crying; only consoled.

When the brother is laid to rest, everyone returns to the clubhouse. The party continues for days. Senior members deliver another eulogy, and a photo of the fallen is hung on the wall. That same photo is sent to every clubhouse across the country, placed in the "forever chapter." A toast is raised.

The atmosphere is unlike any other funeral. Yes, there's sadness, but the overwhelming feeling is one of honour — pride in having been part of his life. There isn't the deep grieving you might expect; instead, the club rallies closer, supporting the brothers and family most affected. Within club culture, a funeral is seen as the pinnacle — the greatest achievement. To die a member and remain in the forever chapter is one of the highest honours. The only comparison I can make is to the Viking belief in Valhalla.

But not everyone is given this honour. In an attempt to save lives, clubs often have a rule: if you take your own life, you are not granted a forever chapter place. No photo on the wall. No club funeral. You are, in fact, removed from the club. Harsh as it sounds, it acts as a deterrent — and for the most part, it works.

WHY MOTORBIKES?

So why motorbikes? They're often seen as rebellious symbols, but for me, they've always been more than that. I've suggested to many people with mental health struggles to get a bike, because riding can temporarily solve a lot of the issues they face. On the flip side, yes, it can be a coping mechanism — but one that's affordable and accessible.

After the war, surplus bikes were cheap and everywhere. The army was practically giving them away. These days, bikes only become expensive once you join a club, because most 1% clubs restrict members to British or American-made bikes. The tradition goes back to wartime — they didn't want to support countries they'd just fought against. It also keeps members uniform.

Non-1% clubs tend to allow any bike, provided it's over 400cc, and usually within the same style (cruiser, sport, etc.). Social Motorcycle Clubs (SMCs) are more relaxed: "We don't care what you ride, as long as you ride." I like that. Though on big rides, similar-paced bikes make things smoother. Smaller-capacity bikes are generally for beginners, restricted by licence anyway.

MOTORCYCLES AND MENTAL HEALTH

The benefits of bikes for mental health are huge:

- Lonely? Get a bike. There's always a group ride happening. Facebook groups are full of them. Pull up anywhere, and people will talk to you about your bike. The opposite sex often takes notice, too.

- Bored? You'll always have a toy to ride, tinker with, or customise.

- Lacking identity? A bike gives you one. Whether it's "rebel," "bad boy," or a community-minded rider on charity runs, it gives you purpose and belonging.

- Need creativity? No two bikes are the same. Customising yours makes it unique, reflecting your personality.

- Struggling emotionally? Go for a ride. The focus required to stay alive clears your head. Riding forces mindfulness. It grounds you, gives you space from your thoughts, and reconnects you with nature.

To this day, 90% of my friends and many of the opportunities that shaped my life came through bikes. That said, you don't need to join a club to enjoy motorcycling. So why do people join? That's something only you can answer.

EVERY TITLE CARRIES WEIGHT

Before you can understand club life, you need to know the different roles people play around it. Not everyone you see in a clubhouse or on a ride is a member. Some are just hanging around, some are trying to earn their place, and others already wear their patch with pride. Every step has its purpose, every stage is a test, and every title carries weight. It's a long road to becoming a full member, and it starts long before you ever put colours on your back.

Hang-around:

A hang-around is someone who isn't a member but literally just hangs around. This is often where the trouble starts. Some hang-arounds are solid — there for the right reasons. But others don't have what it takes to be members, so they act tough, name-drop, and pick fights. It takes years to become a member, so these types usually get weeded out. Think about it: out of thousands of club members, it's usually the same few names in the news. And often, hang-arounds are wrongly labelled as members by the media.

Patch chasers:

These are the female hang-arounds. They're more like groupies, following clubs the way fans follow bands. Patch chasers often bounce from one club to another, always attached to someone in colours. They can cause a lot of drama. Like some of the boys, these women thrive on risk-taking, crave external validation, and avoid facing themselves. Not all are like this, of course — but some are wilder than the men.

It's often asked: *"Does she like me for me, or for the patch?"*

When I first joined, a senior member sat me and the other new guys down. I often joke that it felt like an induction at a workplace. He said:

> *"Now you're in a club, you need to be careful. Girls will throw themselves at you. Old friends will come out of the woodwork. The challenge is knowing who likes you for you, and who just wants something from the patch."*

He was right.

Associates:

These are people who are a little more involved. They might not be members, but they're respected — often connected in the underworld or tough enough to carry weight.

Prospect/Nominee:

Not yet members, but they've put in enough time as hang-arounds (usually five years) to be considered. This stage is "try before you buy," but with limited access.

During this time, you are required to fulfil specific tasks (all clubs are different), but they all require prospects or Nominees to work. A lot of people don't join clubs for this reason, and they constantly use the excuse "I don't want to be a slave or someone's bitch". These people have either not been around a club or don't have what it takes to be a member, because that is not what this time is about.

Yes, you indeed get worked hard. I remember once I was working the bar, cleaning, cooking, picking up members from the airport, and I hadn't slept in a few days, for them to tell me I could go home. The second I had just slipped my toes under the first layer of blankets, my phone rang (it must always be answered). I picked it up to hear "prospect, we miss you, come back now! I pulled myself out of bed, rode the half an hour back to the clubhouse, only to be told to take all the officers' bikes to the petrol station (only 100m away) one by one (about 10) and fill them up, which I did.

As I walked back into the clubhouse, it was all pats on the back. They told me to go home. I said, "Are you serious?" They just smiled and said, "We just wanted to see if you would do it", and sent me on my way. One of the nationals said, "You'll go far in this club," as I angrily walked away, hoping not to receive another call.

You see, this time is to test your inner fortitude and to know if you will go the extra mile for your brothers because it's not what the club can do for you; it's what you can do for the club. Are you going to be a sook and complain when things get a bit tough, or are you going to take it like a man and cop it on the chin to get something you really want?

To break it down even more, why send a new person to meet senior members at the airport? So you and they can meet each other and talk while you're driving them around.

Why work the bar? At the bar, you get to meet and greet every single member, you have to ask them all their names and find out a little bit about them without them having to make a heap of effort and uncomfortable small talk, it's especially handy so the member doesn't have to waste time on a person that might not be around in a few months.

Why would they make you clean the clubhouse? You clean your own house, right? It's no different from your house, and it builds respect and discipline. If you do a shit job or bitch and moan, the members can look at this like, Do we want someone who thinks they are too good and entitled to look after their own house? These people cannot accomplish anything within a specific time frame; how can they be counted on? Everything during this time has a meaning and purpose.

Looking back, it was at this stage that I enjoyed the most. All the long-term members used to say, Don't be in a hurry to get your patch, enjoy this time, and they were right.

I remember three days deep into a party at around 3 am and the national vice president was sweeping the floor, emptying ash trays and bins, basically cleaning like a mad man, I said "let us do that brother", he said "This is my fucking clubhouse bro and ill clean it if I want, anyone that thinks they are too good to clean a clubhouse no matter what position they hold is a piece of shit and doesn't belong in a club, you brothers have done a good job, we have been watching, go and have a bit of fun."

Probationary:

Now, in this step, you are a member, but still have limited access. Like in the first step, you have a new set of duties and different responsibilities, but like the first step, every job is for a reason.

Full member:

Now you're a full member, the real club life begins. For those reading this who are about to get your full patch, stay out of the drama and politics, don't make a mess out of yourself, stay humble, remember your vest isn't bulletproof, and if you see a full ashtray, you are allowed to empty it.

Colours:

This is your vest and patch. It does not touch the ground and is not to be touched by anyone who isn't a member, ever. It's hardearned over a long period of time, and only people who have earned the right and privilege to touch it can. Your vest can not be worn in a car (for most clubs), it stands for motorcycle club and not motorcar club, like some of us used to joke.

Office Bearers:

The ranks and structure originate from the military, with a few modifications. Nationals/State, depending on the club:

- **President:** The boss

- **Vice President:** The boss when the boss is away

- **Sergeant:** Handles any issues outside the club but is mainly a babysitter that looks after the brothers, everyone thinks the sergeant is just there to kick arse, which isn't the case if they are a good sergeant. Most of the time, it's also his job to keep the boys safe and hopefully out of trouble and generally to look after his men.

- **Secretary/Treasurer:** Handles the financial and bookkeeping tasks.

- **Road captain:** is responsible for people on rides the rides themselves, keeping everyone safe and doing the planning.

These same positions also operate at the chapter level.

Life inside a club isn't just about ranks, rides, and patches. Once you've earned your place, it becomes about the world you live in day to day — the clubhouse that's your second home, the women who stand beside the brothers, the rules about leaving, and the traditions that tie everyone together. This is where club culture really comes alive.

Clubhouse:

The clubhouse is the sanctuary. It's the members' fortress of solitude — a place where everyone knows your name and you're in a safe, non-judgmental environment. It's where you party, where you live if needed, and where you hold church (meetings). It's meant to be a safe space, though the reality can sometimes be the opposite, especially if you're not a member.

Clubhouses can be a lot of fun, but never forget: people have been killed in them. The clubhouse I was in was set on fire, shot up, blown up — and someone was killed there. Someone was also killed at another local chapter. Yet somehow, for the most part, I still felt safe. The irony isn't lost on me — feelings don't always match facts, and cognitive dissonance is real.

The walls are usually covered in photos of past members, their stories passed down from brother to brother. Clubhouses themselves can be anything from a shed to a house, to elaborate bars that rival gentlemen's clubs — built with the blood, sweat, and tears of members past and present, and decorated with memorabilia from other chapters.

We used to joke that the clubhouse gives you what you need. Feeling lonely? Go to the clubhouse and a brother will turn up. Need to escape life for a while? Head to the clubhouse. Want to catch up with mates? Go to the clubhouse and see what's happening. Missus kicked you out and you've got nowhere to stay? Off to the clubhouse. In some countries, you're even required to live at the clubhouse for a set period.

When I talk to ex-members now, they all say the same thing: they miss the clubhouse. It wasn't just a building; it became the centre point for everything in life. It also kept members and the community safer — instead of being out in town getting into trouble, brothers were together, tucked away. Going into town as a patched member is a whole different story, with its own set of rules.

Old Lady:

In Australia, this term doesn't carry the same weight as it does overseas. Aussie women don't like being called "old." But in clubs, it simply means the partner of a brother. Side chicks, patch chasers, and new girlfriends don't get this title. It's reserved for long-term girlfriends and wives.

Overseas, this can come with another label that drives Aussie girls mad: *Property of Patch.*

Here, most women won't wear those. However, it's not meant to be ownership in the way outsiders perceive it. It's actually a term of endearment — a way of saying this woman isn't just another girl hanging around. She's a wife, a partner, someone important who deserves respect and protection. She's earned her place.

Some clubs even have kids' patches and vests for members' children — but only blood, not stepkids.

Standings:

When people leave a club, it's usually defined as *good standings* or *bad standings.*

- **Good Standing**: You leave on good terms. You're welcome back for visits, can remain friends, and even rejoin later if you wish.

- **Bad Standing**: The harshest version, in the old days, meant total bans on communication, fines, having your bike taken, or even being "bashed on sight." Nowadays, it's often less extreme — usually being cut off, maybe fined, depending on what laws were broken. Unfortunately, most departures end up being bad standings.

Many people think once you're in, you can't get out. However, the truth is that members do leave. A photo on the clubhouse wall might be up one year — and gone two years later.

Christmas:

Club Christmas parties were a highlight. Like most families, we had Santa, presents, and a kids' section of the day. After that, the adults partied for days.

Clubs even made their own Christmas cards. We loved receiving them from around the world, seeing familiar faces, spotting new ones, catching up with the global brotherhood. We'd sit around looking at those cards for ages.

They often had two extra sections that the public never saw: one for brothers in jail, and one for those who were absent. But you'd better have a damn good reason to be absent.

Club life is full of contradictions. It's a world built on **love, loyalty, and respect**, but also one riddled with **hate, drama, and lies**. These are the members, and these are their stories...

CHAPTER FOUR

THE SOCIAL MOTORCYCLE CLUB (SMC) MEMBER PERSPECTIVE

Birol Ozturk – Founder of Wanderers Social Motorcycle Club - 53 years old

Question 1. What prompted you to join a motorcycle club? What bike did you ride?

I was drawn to the sense of community and brotherhood that comes with riding with others who share a passion for motorcycles. I was also interested in the social aspects — the group rides and events. At the time, I was riding a Harley-Davidson Night Rod.

Question 2. What was your experience in a social motorcycle club like? Were you only in the one club?

At first, I didn't join a club but supported other social clubs by joining their rides. I really valued the small group of friends I made through those rides, and before long, we were riding together every weekend. Eventually, I decided to start my own social motorcycle club, which I named the Wanderers SMC.

Question 3. Why did you choose an SMC over a 1% club?

For me, choosing a social motorcycle club over a 1% club came down to different priorities and values. SMCs emphasise friendship, group rides, and social events, without the same level of commitment and exclusivity found in 1% clubs.

I was more interested in the social aspect of motorcycling than the intense — and sometimes confrontational — elements of 1% clubs. Those clubs often have stricter membership requirements, including heavy time commitments and strict codes of conduct. SMCs offer a more relaxed environment, where members can enjoy riding and socialising without the same demands. That aligned better with my values.

Question 4. Do you think your childhood or upbringing influenced you to join a club?

I grew up in a close-knit group of about 10 to 15 neighbourhood friends. Every day after school, we played soccer, tennis, cricket and football — always together. It gave me a strong appreciation for being part of a social group.

That background made me comfortable with clubs and group activities. So, when I started riding, joining a motorcycle club felt like a natural extension of my childhood — it was a way to share adventures and experiences with more people. The group rides resonated with those memories of energetic, playful days.

Question 5. What did you get out of being in a motorcycle club that you were missing in your own life?

At the time, I was missing a strong sense of belonging. The club gave me a tight-knit group of friends who shared my interests and values. Being part of a club let me fully immerse myself in my passion for motorcycling and connect with others who shared the same enthusiasm.

Question 6. How did it benefit your life?

Motorcycling gave me a sense of freedom and exhilaration. The open road, the wind — it's liberating. It provided an escape from daily routines and responsibilities, almost therapeutic.

Being part of a club introduced me to new friends whom I would have never met otherwise. That sense of belonging enriched my social life and gave me lasting friendships. Riding also meant exploring new places and having adventures that I would have never experienced otherwise.

It helped me grow, learn new skills, overcome challenges, and gain confidence. All of that improved my mental well-being.

Question 7. How did it hinder your life?

The main negative was stereotypes. Some people misunderstood what being in a club meant. I lost a couple of old friends because I had less time for them — my priorities had shifted to club life.

But the trade-off was worth it. I gained happiness, purpose, and self-worth through the new friendships and experiences.

Question 8. Do you have any standout stories or experiences?

I'll save those for potential podcasts.

Question 9. Is there really a brotherhood — a code of loyalty?

Yes. In many clubs, there's a strong emphasis on support — whether it's practical, like helping with repairs or rides, or emotional support during tough times. But this is most evident while you're an active member.

When you leave, even in good standing, you often lose that close connection. It's like leaving a job — those friendships fade over time. Understandable, but still disheartening.

Question 10. What advice would you give to someone joining a bike club for the first time?

- Research clubs in your area — each has its own culture, values, and activities.

- Find one that aligns with your interests and expectations.

- Understand the time, effort, and sometimes financial commitment involved.

- Be prepared to actively participate, support fellow members, and respect the group's code of conduct.

- Build genuine relationships — brotherhood is central to many clubs.

- Embrace diversity — every club has a range of personalities and perspectives.

- Be adaptable. Membership dynamics can change.

Above all, remember why you wanted to join in the first place: to enjoy riding and share your passion with others.

Question 11. How was life after stepping back from a bike club?

It can leave a void. Going from an active club life to a quieter routine feels abrupt. For me, it wasn't too hard because my priorities had shifted. Becoming a parent gave me new responsibilities and joys, and that filled the gap.

Question 12. Would you join a club again?

Absolutely. I have no regrets. The decade I spent in the club was rewarding. The friendships, the experiences, the connections — I truly value them.

Question 13. How is your life now after spending time away from club life?

I feel satisfied, knowing I gave it my all.

Question 14. Have you ever been diagnosed with mental health issues?

No.

Question 15. Do you regret joining a bike club?

No.

Question 16. Do you still see anyone from your bike club days?

I catch up on the phone.

Question 17. How did being in a club shape you as a person?

It gave me new perspectives, taught me to value the journey as much as the destination, and helped me appreciate different viewpoints. It enriched my life with skills, relationships, and balance.

Question 18. How did you handle the image and identity of being a club member?

I loved it. Being part of a community, contributing, organising rides and events — it was fulfilling.

Question 19. What do you think of 1% clubs from an SMC perspective? Should you be allowed a back patch?

SMCs focus on riding, community, and camaraderie. 1% clubs are more intense and exclusive. There's generally mutual respect between the two, but they play different roles.

The back patch in a 1% club is a serious symbol, tied to values, tradition, and commitment. For SMCs, wearing one wouldn't be appropriate — it could cause misunderstanding or conflict.

A common misconception is that all 1% clubs are criminal or dangerous. While some may have controversial reputations, many members are simply passionate motorcyclists with loyalty and tradition at their core.

Both 1% clubs and SMCs offer community and brotherhood, just in different ways. Respect for each club's culture is essential.

Question 20. Anything you'd like to add?

Overall, motorcycle clubs create a positive, social environment where riders connect, share their passion, and enrich their lives through camaraderie and experience.

FROM HANG-AROUND TO SOCIAL CLUB PRESIDENT

(Anonymous) - aged 66

Question 1. What prompted me to hang around 1% clubs?

When growing up and riding dirt bikes, some of my friends' older brothers were involved with — or members of — clubs which may have been 1% clubs or single-patch clubs. That started an interest around the age of 12. I found it fascinating to listen to them talk about the parties and rides they'd done on the weekends, so it was a natural tendency as I got older to seek out these older brothers and start hanging out with them in the hope of getting an invite to some of their events.

At this stage, riding with them was out of the question as I was unlicensed, still riding dirt, and only around 15 years old. But I did get an invite to a party.

I was already a seasoned drinker at the ripe old age of 15 and was excited to attend. The party itself was nothing new — just a big fire in a paddock in the middle of nowhere, like I'd done plenty of times. I was able to get there on my dirt bike through farmland and the occasional country road.

On arrival, after hiding my dirt bike half a kilometre away, I walked into the party feeling a bit insecure until the bloke who gave me the invite spoke to me and took me up to the makeshift bar. That's when I knew I wanted that lifestyle — the barmaid was topless. Not the first pair of tits I'd ever seen, but after the initial shock, I looked around and saw four or five half-naked girls and one totally naked. That became the beginning of no return for me.

Question 2. What was your experience like hanging around a 1% club?

Overall, my experiences have been varied as each club can be seen or defined differently. Over the many years of knocking around with 1% clubs, I could tell a million stories. A lot of the clubs I hung out with no longer exist, and many of the people I knew in those clubs have died. It wouldn't be a lie to say that, other than one event, all my years were positive.

The one bad experience was a run-in with a nom or a prospect who took a dislike to me at an event at the clubhouse. Things may have escalated if it wasn't for a patched member friend taking us both aside and laying down the law. The rest of my interactions, on the whole, have been positive experiences.

Question 3. How did the experience shape who you are now?

I've never really thought about how it has shaped who I am, because I have been loath to look internally. I can be somewhat loopy and have not-so-nice thoughts going through my head. But as I said, I'll do this honestly, so I'll try to give as close to the truth as I dare.

Being on the periphery of 1% clubs has given me the opportunity to mix and socialise with mostly like-minded individuals who exist on both sides of the law. For the most part, their law-breaking is traffic-related and the occasional bashing of someone who has been disrespectful to a club or a person attached to a club, or on a few occasions, in the protection of children. Watching them gave me an understanding of life. Combined with having one foot on either side of the fence regarding the law, it has given me a life perspective that few are able to achieve. It also gave me the confidence I never had growing up.

Question 4. Do you think your childhood or certain events in your upbringing led you to join a club?

Without a doubt, there were events in my childhood that made me lean towards club life. Firstly, I was raised in an army background and was always searching for the comradeship and belonging my father spoke of — the kind he experienced during his war years and his army career, which spanned 26 years and another 28 working as a civilian for the army.

I had only ever participated in team sports, and the friendships there were fleeting as teams changed personnel from year to year.

The other major factor was being sexually abused from the age of 8 to around 11 or 12 by a relative. That left me feeling weak, vulnerable, and defenceless. As I got older, I think maybe I was looking for someone or something that offered protection. Looking back now, it feels selfish — I should have done something to protect myself. Later in life, I did: training with some friends in a 1% club, getting married, and having children gave me the strength to learn to defend myself.

Question 5. What do you think you got out of hanging around a motorcycle club that you were missing in your own life?

For me, that's an easy one: I got that brotherhood my father had, and I've made lifelong friendships. I gained the ability to connect with people who are like-minded but also very diverse in origin, personality, beliefs, and vocation.

Just as an example, some of the bikers I've met in 1% clubs have been lawyers, religious ministers, politicians, and defence personnel. But in both social and 1% clubs, we all had that binding love of motorcycles and adventure.

Going to club events played a major part in my adult life. 1% parties — unless you've been to one, it's hard to describe. They can be raunchy or relaxed, but rarely have any trouble. Social club rallies are something else altogether, with gymkhanas on the bikes and vast numbers of friends you just haven't met yet, many of whom ride hundreds of kilometres every year to the same rally. In short, I found happiness there that I never found anywhere else.

Question 6. How did it benefit your life?

I think the benefits are far-reaching and, in my case, very personal. The practical benefits were the contacts you make. Meet a lawyer or an accountant? You can ask for advice. Know a builder or bricklayer? They'll help with a project. I've had 1%ers lend me bobcats, fix my bike, and babysit my kids — all at no cost. Fringe benefits, you could say.

On a personal level, I've cried in the arms of a 1%er and wasn't judged. At my baby son's funeral, an entourage of twenty men turned up in suits, wearing their colours, on their bikes. They showed support and compassion not just to my wife and me, but to our family and friends, offering words of condolence and comfort. One of the saddest days of my life was also uplifting. My family, who had always been afraid of bikers, saw that day that they weren't what the media or their own preconceptions made them out to be. They were supportive, caring people.

Question 7. How did it hinder your life?

Having never been a 1%er, it didn't overly hinder my life. Some friends and family were vocal about the "big bad bikers" leading me astray, but I think they had it all wrong. There have been nights in clubhouses across four states where I was the one with more convictions than anyone else in the room. Who would've thought that an old fart like me could "outlaw" better than an outlaw biker? Beggars belief.

Question 8. Any standout stories or experiences?

There are too many, but I'll share a couple.

One was riding my old '74 Shovelhead Super Glide on a run, stuck behind some prospects whose bikes were falling apart. Along the way, I picked up a foot peg, a tail light, and a number plate from their bikes — only to lose most of them again before we arrived. On the way back, we had some fun leapfrogging on the road. A patched mate came up beside me, reached over, turned off my bike, pulled my key out, and threw it into the grass. He thought it was hilarious. At the time, I didn't — but looking back, it's a funny memory.

Another was being asked to help roll joints — half a pound of pot into three-paper cones — with a nom and another hang-around to prepare for a national run. That was an all-day job.

I've also been fortunate to meet famous people in clubhouses. George Thorogood, Kim Wilde, Wendy James from Transvision Vamp, and Wilbur Wilde from *Hey Hey It's Saturday* are some that come to mind.

Question 9. Is there a brotherhood, a code of loyalty?

Definitely, it's as real as any other close-knit group, even like what soldiers experience. It may not be forged in the same way, but the bond is genuine. The only thing that breaks it is betrayal — either by word or by deed.

Question 10. What advice would you give to someone wanting to hang around a club?

The biggest piece of advice: be yourself. Don't pretend to be something you're not, because you'll get found out. I once knew a bloke who was trying to prospect but got caught out. Things went down, and he bolted, leaving a couple of brothers to be bashed. He never got patched.

Also, get to know the older members. They're usually the ones who decide who stays and who goes. They can also be the most understanding and willing to give advice. If you give it a go, give it your best shot. The rewards outweigh the bullshit.

Question 11. What was life like after leaving a club?

The ending of our social club was one of the toughest times of my life. It left me broken, worried, and full of self-doubt. I had often asked myself if I would take a bullet for the club and never answered. We were pressured into shutting down by a much larger club. We had potential to grow, but maybe that was our undoing.

Later, I was able to find happiness in another social club that had been established for years. It was family-friendly and gave me back a sense of belonging.

Question 12. Would you hang around or join another club?

I already have. I still attend 1% shows, poker runs, and other events. I don't visit clubhouses just to drink anymore, but I do still go to parties. Once it's in your blood, it's hard to walk away.

Question 13. How is life now after some time out of club life?

I'm still in a social club and still enjoy the lifestyle. I've never been a patch chaser — I'm a lifestyle chaser. I'll admit, I'm just an average rider, but I've always been good at partying. Bring on the next rally.

Question 14. Have you ever been diagnosed with mental health issues?

Yes. I was diagnosed with depression in the 1970s following the abuse I went through. I was heavily medicated, which I hated. The meds stopped the highs and lows, but they also stopped everything else. I stopped taking them and found my solace in my dirt bike.

I skipped school to ride dirt, dodging the police if caught. Alcohol and drugs followed, but eventually I chose bikes over oblivion. To this day, I still suffer from depression, but the lifestyle, rallies, and rides pull me back. I try to focus on the positives in life. That's my way of dealing with it.

Question 15. Did you get help pre-, during, or post-club life?

Only during the early years. I never liked medication, so now I rely on recognising when depression comes creeping back and focus on my own awareness to deal with it. Abuse never leaves you — you just learn to live with it.

Question 16. Did you always feel safe as a hang-around?

Mostly, yes. Safer in some ways than in the outside world. But there was always a small fear of saying or doing something wrong. One drunken mistake could get you banished. And being banished meant losing everything: the people, the lifestyle, the brotherhood. That fear kept me on my toes.

Question 17. Do you still see anyone from your old club days?

Yes, I do, but not as much as I used to. Priorities change with age — marriage, kids, business. But I know many of them miss it, even if they don't say it out loud. I encourage them to get back on the bike, even if it's just for social riding or mentoring.

Question 18. How did club life shape you as a person?

Without a doubt, motorcycles saved my life. Without bike life, I don't think I'd still be here. To me, it's not so much about *club life* as it is *bike life*. A club can't exist without bikes, but bikes exist without clubs. Bikes make us who we are.

Question 19. Why didn't you ever step up to join a 1% club?

Fear. I didn't think I had enough to offer. I wasn't a fighter, and I didn't think I was tough enough. Family played a big part too — marriage and kids were my priority.

Over the years, I was asked to join four different 1% clubs. I don't know if I ever had the potential to become a 1%er, but my own insecurities and circumstances prevented it.

Question 20. Is club life really like *Sons of Anarchy*?

No. That's TV drama. Sure, there are enforcers and controlled violence when necessary, but not the constant shootouts and drama you see on screen.

I never saw organised gun-running or drug trafficking. In fact, I've seen more drug dealers in football clubs than in motorcycle clubs. Women were never forced to do anything against their will — they were there because they wanted to be.

Most of the time, members are just regular blokes doing regular things — they just happen to ride bikes and have a brotherhood outsiders will never fully understand.

Question 21. Anything else you'd like to add?

I'd like to thank every club and every person I've crossed paths with. The memories, advice, and friendships I've gained have helped me through some of the best and worst times of my life.

So my final word is this: **ride hard, ride soft, ride wherever the road leads — just ride.** For me, bikes are as important as food, water, and air.

And maybe, just maybe, one day the old clubs that were beaten out or swallowed up will rise again. With the right push and maybe political representation, the fraternity could stand united. There are a lot of us out there.

CHAPTER SIX

THE SECOND GENERATION

Question 1. What prompted you to join a motorcycle club? What bike did you ride?

I joined a motorcycle club because it was normal in my life. My dad was a 1%er, my stepfather was a 1%er, and I had other extended relatives in 1% motorcycle clubs. From a very young age, I saw being in a 1% club as normal. It was brotherhood and family to me. The people living next door, down the road, and so on — they were the different and weird ones.

From the time I was 5, I knew I wanted to be a member of the club. I even prepared my now wife when she was 15 (I was 16 at the time), telling her I would be a member one day. I grew up with my mother and stepfather, whom I never saw as a stepfather — he was just my father. I spent a lot of time around the club he was in and looked up to the members as role models.

As I grew older, I found I didn't fit in many places. I was always waiting to get a bike. Eventually, I bought a new 2006 FXST Harley-Davidson and joined my stepfather's 1% motorcycle club at the age of 22. This actually broke a deal I had made at 14 with another member — that I would join by 21. We had even tried to figure out ways to get me in earlier, on a learner's licence at 16, but I decided to wait.

Question 2. What was your experience in a 1% motorcycle club like? Were you only in the one club?

When I first joined, a member told me that in the club there would be good times and bad times, and the bad times would seem to outweigh the good — but it was the good times that counted.

I really took this on board, and it sums up club life well. We had a lot of good times. We partied for days, starting Friday nights, and had a ball doing it. But outside of that, there was the serious side of club politics.

I was only in one club, but I was in multiple chapters. I started as a nominee in a chapter in Western Sydney. Then, during my second meeting as a member, without my knowledge, a group of members I was close with announced they were starting a new chapter. They got up and left — and I got up and left with them. (This turned out to be a test, which I passed.) We started another chapter in Southern Sydney, and eventually, a group of us started another chapter on the South Coast of NSW. That was always my goal from before joining, since it was my home.

Question 3. How did the experience shape who you are now?

I have left the club life behind, but it played a big part in my life. Leaving the club has left a void I can't fill — trust me, I've tried.

Question 4. Do you think your childhood or certain events in your upbringing led you to join a club?

Definitely, my childhood was spent with frequent visits to clubhouses and going on national runs on the back of a bike, from a young child up to a teenager. I used to wait all year for the annual show the club put on, or the national run. We even had Christmas parties for the children at the clubhouse. Everyone I looked up to as a child was a 1%er.

Question 5. What do you think you got out of being in a motorcycle club that you were missing in your own life?

Belonging somewhere. I never fitted in amongst normal society. I bounced from group to group as a kid, but always with the kids who had it tough.

By the age of 14, I was already going to Kings Cross, getting into clubs, and attending pubs and clubs locally. Being in the club gave me structured brotherhood, consistent people to be around, rules, and a sense of being king of the streets I grew up on.

Question 6. How did it benefit your life?

It gave me a sense of belonging. I got to be part of something with some seriously solid blokes who would do anything for you — and that has stuck with me.

Question 7. How did it hinder your life?

Members were getting involved in my personal life. For example, one time a member rang me during the day while I was sleeping for the night shift. When I told him I was sleeping, he had a go at me. It turned into an argument, and a higher-ranking member had to get involved to solve it. The outcome was that I ended up giving them a safe time to call me, so they wouldn't ruin my sleep for work. I can't stay awake 24/7 just in case of a phone call.

It also took a toll on my marriage, as it does with many married club members. The constant partying, the secrecy, not being able to tell her club business, and going out without explanation. My chapter was strict about not involving women — we were lucky to invite our wives to one party a year. I'm lucky my wife stood by me, but it took a long time to heal.

Question 8. Do you have any standout stories or experiences?

On one of my first rides as a member, we took a lap around Western Sydney with about 50 members. A nominee at the back of the pack did a big burnout, not realising there was a patrol car behind us. The red and blues came on, and we took off.

The closer we got to the clubhouse, the more patrol cars joined the chase. We ended up with a fleet of them. Once back, we locked the gate behind us. A couple of members had to park out front and come in through the gate. We refused to talk to the police.

While I was standing at the gate with a high-ranking member, a big old police sergeant walked up the driveway and asked whose bike was in the driveway. Silence. Then he said, "What happened to the days you all painted your colours on your bikes?" It was then that we realised we were about to get away with the chase. After some conversation, the sergeant told the others, "These blokes do this every Friday night. They've done it for decades. Leave them alone and go home." And that was the end of it.

Question 9. Is there really a brotherhood or code of loyalty?

I felt I had it at one point, but I think I lost it along the way. I don't think I ever really got what I was after, except with a few members. I also think my undiagnosed mental health issues didn't help. It's hard to make sound decisions and maintain close brotherhood when you're out of touch with reality.

Question 10. What would you say to people wishing to join a bike club for the first time?

Don't. Do something more constructive — maybe join the military or build a family and a career. If that doesn't work and you feel like you have no other choice, hang out with a club you know. See what they're like and if you can see yourself doing it at least twice a week with those people. Trust me, you'll get close with them, and if it doesn't work out, things can get messy.

Question 11. How was your life after leaving a bike club, and how did you get out?

I felt like I lost my identity. I had to live life with so-called normal people. I've since learned that just because someone isn't in a gang doesn't mean they're a good person.

I left the club after an unsuccessful attempt at starting another chapter in a remote mining town where I was living and working. Ultimately, there were multiple reasons I left, which I talk more about in Question 18.

Question 12. Would you ever consider joining a club again?

No. I want to set the right example for my kids. I don't want them to think that being in a 1% club is the right thing to do.

Question 13. How is your life now after some time away from club life?

Good. I have an awesome wife, fantastic kids, a home, and an evolving career.

Question 14. Have you ever been diagnosed with mental health issues?

Yes. I was first diagnosed with transient psychotic disorder with a mood component while still in the club, after at least 18 months in psychosis, before I got treatment. I didn't realise I was unwell. Being a 1%er with untreated mental health conditions was quite challenging. That's when I learned to mask my symptoms.

Since then, I've been diagnosed with delusional disorder, and now with schizoaffective disorder (depressive type).

Question 15. Did you get help for these pre-, post-, or during club life?

It's highly possible I had mental health issues before club life, but I never got help. I started treatment while still in the club, and I still receive treatment now. It will be ongoing for life.

Question 16. Do you regret joining a bike club?

Nope. I wouldn't change my past, as I wouldn't be where I am today.

Question 17. Do you still see anyone from your bike club days?

Yes.

Question 18. How do you feel being in a bike club helped mould you into the person you are today? What cool things are you doing now?

That's hard to answer, because I don't think the club made me who I am today. When I went through psychosis, I was in it so long I asked my doctors to break it down. They said, "You've had the equivalent of a significant head injury causing brain damage, and it will take time to heal."

That changed me. So did having kids, staying loyal to my wife of 24 years and the mother of my children, and building my career. All of these changes led me to leave the club behind.

Some of the cool things I'm doing now: I've been a leader for a global mining giant and for a global transport company. I'm now pursuing a career outside people management in a global transport company.

Question 19. How did you handle gaining the image/identity of being a club member, and then losing it again?

That was a hard one. It happened gradually as I moved away from where I grew up — where everyone knew me and knew I was a member. Moving to a remote mining town, I got in with local friends and families. They treated me like one of them. That's where I learned to live without the club.

I eventually left while living in that mining town. But honestly, I miss putting on my cut and going for a pack ride. Losing that identity wasn't without hurt.

Question 20. Is it really like *Sons of Anarchy*? Any misconceptions or truths you'd like to share?

I never got into *Sons of Anarchy*. But it still makes my blood boil seeing someone wear one of those patches in public after what I went through to earn mine.

Question 21. Anything you'd like to add, elaborate, or summarise with?

I joined a motorcycle club and left a gang.

Regards,
Jake

PARTNER PERSPECTIVE

Kerry age 48

Did you know anything about motorcycle clubs before becoming a partner of a member and, if so, what?

Not a real lot — just had friends in clubs and had hung out in clubhouses for parties previously. Clubs weren't really in the media when I was growing up, and it was exciting when you did see a club ride come through your hometown.

Did you only date one person who was a member of a motorcycle club? If multiple, were they from different clubs, and how did they differ?

Only one — and I'm now married to him. Seven years married, thirteen together.

How did the experience shape who you are now?

It really opened my eyes to the way the media and the public think and act towards 1%ers. I come from a strict/straight family, and they were devastated when I started hanging with 1%ers. I had a birthday party at the clubhouse and invited my family — from that day on, their attitudes changed for the positive, with my grandfather (bless him) absolutely interested in the lifestyle and loving having a beer with the boys. He especially loved that everyone looked after everyone, and members took care of him at the party and then afterwards, when he needed a hand around the yard, etc.

Do you think your childhood or certain events in your upbringing led you to be attracted to that lifestyle?

I've always been the black sheep in my family and always the rebel while growing up. I feel I was attracted due to the "no care what others think" idea.

What did you get out of being part of the motorcycle club world that you were missing in your own life?

Excitement — something exciting to do. Cool weekends riding all over the countryside.

How did it benefit your life?

I founded a youth organisation over 10 years ago — the lived experience from living with outlaws gives me "credibility" with young people in the justice system to feel they can trust me and my staff. The young people coming out of detention who pretend to be gangsters love to hang out, hear old stories, see how successful my husband is in his own business, and chat with him about how to change their lifestyles to become successful.

How did it hinder your life?

Only a little. We went travelling years ago, and my husband was told he was unable to travel due to being a known member of a criminal outlaw group. He has no criminal record but was still detained at the airport. Another time, when I first founded the youth organisation, I met with a highly ranked politician (still current) to discuss my plans for young people in my region. I'll never forget what he said to me, "You are creating a space to recruit young people into outlaw gangs!" LOL!!! That same politician now funds our organisation to create positive pathways for young people and has had to publicly announce over $1,000,000 in funding for us. Just today, he sent a support letter for funding this year.

Do you have any standout stories or experiences you'd like to expand on?

- *Bikie harassed by police @ March in March* — this is from a protest rally I attended when Campbell Newman was bringing in outlaw laws. My husband was coming to pick me up from the rally when the police tried to pull him over for wearing his colours.

- *Queensland girl who woke to armed police in bedroom 'feared for her life'* — this happened to us at home after the protest rally.

- *Outlaw funerals* — I've been to many. What a top send-off!

Is there really a brotherhood or code/loyalty?

Definitely when it came to club vs club, but, from my experience, members were happy to secretly "stack the deck" within their own club to secure whatever motive at the time. It was a weekly thing with phone calls and coffee catch-ups before weekly church.

What would you say to people wishing to date someone in a bike club for the first time?

Back then, go for it and enjoy the ride. Today — do your homework on your love interest and club, and be prepared for excessive police attention.

How was your life initially after leaving the bike club world, and how did you get out?

Worrying. There were threats of violence, money to be paid, bikes to be taken, and paraphernalia to be returned. But nothing ever came of it. To this day, hubby can run into a member at the shops, etc., and there's no drama. We still often catch up with long-term members for a beer and BBQ.

Would you ever consider the club lifestyle again, and were there certain fears or worries that came with being a partner of a member?

Not anymore. We decided to leave years ago when it all became too hard to belong. We have kids and grandkids, and it just wasn't worth the hassle of police harassment, not travelling, and being under the microscope. I was never threatened personally, but I was in the clubhouse one night when shots were fired into the house. The boys were super quick at getting all of us out and home. My main concern actually came from police — being raided, questioned, or police coming to our home or workplace.

How is your life now after some time away from that life?

Amazing — we can travel, we can go to local restaurants, we don't have to plan our days around club runs, and we don't wonder when the police might come again.

Have you ever been diagnosed with mental health issues? If so, can you elaborate?

Nope.

Did you get help for these pre-, post-, or during club life?

—

Do you regret being the partner of a bikie? Reasons?

I don't regret any part of my life — it has made me who I am today, and I'm comfortable with that.

Do you still see anyone from those days, and how did the other females in the club feel about each other and navigate the bikie world? Was there drama/hierarchy?

The president's wife liked to think she had some sort of authority, but that wasn't the case. Other than that, most partners were really cool girls. I never saw any drama between the girls and still have many of them as close girlfriends. A lot from our chapter members have now separated from their partners but still remain close with me and others. Most don't speak to the president's wife, though.

How do you feel being in the bike club environment helped mould you into the person you are today? Tell us the cool things you're doing with your life.

Growing up around the bike club environment taught me loyalty, strength, and resilience. It shaped who I am today and gave me the confidence to stand strong in every part of my life. Those experiences taught me the value of community and standing by your word. I am now doing so many great things and living a life I am proud of. I'm involved in leadership, mentoring, and community development, helping others find purpose and direction. Life is full, meaningful, and moving forward in ways I never imagined.

How did you handle getting the image/fame/identity of being the partner of a member and then losing it again?

I'm probably more recognised now. I share my story if appropriate.

Is it really like *Sons of Anarchy*? Any misconceptions or truths you'd like to discuss?

Haha — everyone asks this question. All I can say is there was never anyone who looked like Jax in our chapter.

Anything you'd like to finish, add, elaborate, or summarise with?

Heaps and heaps more stories to share if you want more. xx

THE FULL PATCH MEMBER

What prompted you to join a motorcycle club? What bike did you ride?

From the area I grew up in and hanging out with boys from another OMCG that were making money and getting girls — they were living the dream life, I thought. Driving nice cars and doing whatever the fuck they wanted. No boss, everything was on their time.

I rode a Harley Davidson Dyna Wide Glide and a V-Rod.

What was your experience in a 1% motorcycle club like? Were you only in the one club?

My experience had a lot of high and low points. I joined an Australian-based 1% club in my early 20s, which was a bad experience, as I was given my colours after 2 months as vice president. This definitely got to my head, and I ended up on a national run, blind drunk, turning on other members from other chapters and getting myself booted then and there.

I was left in a hotel room with nothing, in a different state, and having to fly home alone scared shitless.

I then joined another worldwide OMCG. Here, I did my time as a prospect for 12 months, hanging around, doing my dues, and visiting every charter around Australia before being signed off by the president of each chapter. This was a great experience and I loved doing it. I thought I had found my place and brothers.

How did the experience shape who you are now?

To be honest, I don't know, other than teaching me to stand up for myself. But the good and bad experiences have caused me anxiety and sometimes make me think about the stupid shit I did. It taught me to be a man and take ownership and responsibility for everything I have done.

Do you think your childhood or certain events in your upbringing led you to join a club?

Probably. I was always thinking I wasn't good enough growing up for my old man. I felt like he treated my younger brother a lot easier than he did me, so it was like I had to prove something to myself.

What do you think you got out of being in a motorcycle club that you were missing in your own life?

A solid brotherhood. Everyone was even and respected each other. No one was better than anyone else, and we were all fkn men.

I had a tight group of mates growing up, but at the time of joining, the majority of them were all lost and fkd on drugs. I was missing that connection and definitely found it in the second OMCG I joined.

How did it benefit your life?

To be honest, it didn't — but I had to see that for myself.

How did it hinder your life?

I wasn't known to the police prior to joining, but then I had a target on my name from regular travelling with the club, repping colours, and being pulled over for consorting. I was then arrested and charged for something I didn't do, and spent copious amounts of money and years on bail/parole.

I was served an FPO, allowing Raptor the right to raid my house without a warrant, to date, three times. I was flogged by Raptor after they kicked my door down while I was asleep — guns raised, fully suited. I was left with 500 hours of community service and daily sign-in at the local police station, 30 minutes away. More time in court, more money wasted, until I could prove my innocence.

Do you have any standout stories or experiences you would like to tell and expand on?

No. I will never talk about anything like that.

What would you say to people wishing to join a bike club for the first time?

Take a good, hard look at it and make sure this is something you really want. You will be targeted by the police, no doubt. Think about the repercussions for your family. Not only does it cause harm to you, but it also causes harm to your wife and kids.

How was your life initially after leaving a bike club, and how did you get out?

I was anxious as fuck. I had words with a high-ranking member from another club over messages and was therefore booted.

Would you ever consider joining a club again?

It's gone over my head multiple times — but no, not in Australia.

How is your life now after some time away from club life?

Life is good, but I still deal with mental health issues to this day.

Did you receive help for these issues during, before, or after club life?

Yes, after being flogged by Raptor.

Do you regret joining a bike club?

Fuck no. I don't regret anything.

Do you still see anyone from your bike club days?

I've caught up a couple of times, but not frequently.

How do you feel being in a bike club helped mould you into the person you are today? Tell us the cool things you're doing with your life.

I now do NDIS support work and have for the last 2 years, working with troubled youth and special needs, giving back where I can. I do online coaching, no fake shit, I am me, straight to the point. I've never changed.

Is it really like being in Sons of Anarchy? Any misconceptions or truths you would like to discuss?

I don't watch those TV shows. I'm sure there is some truth to it, but mostly it's fake.

Anything you would like to finish, add, elaborate or summarise with?

There will always be good and bad in everything — from a football club, to a soccer club, to a motorcycle club. If this is what you're set on, then fkn do it. If you're second-guessing it, I suggest you join a social club where the rules aren't so strict and leaving or getting booted isn't going to cause you serious harm, money, or mental illness.

CHAPTER NINE

EX-PRESIDENT, STREET GANG MEMBER, AND SECOND-GENERATION MEMBER

Jacob Little, *age 34*

What prompted you to join a motorcycle club? What bike did you ride?

Joining a club for me was something that was ingrained from a young age.

Ever since I was a boy, I grew up seeing my dad ride bikes and be involved in the club. It wasn't something he brought home too much, but it was definitely in my life. As I got older, I was looking for brotherhood and family. My dad was taken away from me at 10 years old to serve a 16-and-a-half-year prison sentence. So, I grew up around jail — having jail phone calls, my mates in jail, and eventually I went to jail myself. During my incarceration, I met a member of the same club my father was in, and it started to become more and more appealing to me.

What was your experience in a 1% motorcycle club like? Were you only in the one club?

My experience in an outlaw motorcycle club was that there were a lot more bad times than good times. But the good times were a lot of fun. I enjoyed the brotherhood, hanging out with the boys at the clubhouse, the women, the parties, the riding with my brothers, getting fucked up on drugs and alcohol, and having big benders.

But included in that was a lot of politics, which I don't like now, didn't like then, and I don't think I ever will. That's life though, and it happens everywhere — in every organisation.

I was only in one club, but I was also president of that chapter, as well as the leader of a street gang.

How did the experience shape who you are now?

I feel like my experience shaped me to be the man I am today. Without jail and being involved with gangs, I wouldn't have some of the skills I have now. I learned to read the room, pick up on who's talking shit, and see who has real dash and sticks to their word. In any area of life — business, underworld crime, or the bikie lifestyle — that's very important.

Do you think your childhood or certain events in your upbringing led you to join a club?

I definitely don't think I would have ended up joining a gang if my father weren't in one. Otherwise, I may never have had the exposure. Maybe I still could have, since I grew up in housing commission with a lot of domestic violence. But visiting my dad and having that life become normal definitely gave me a big push.

What do you think you got out of being in a motorcycle club that you were missing in your own life?

I don't think I got anything out of the motorcycle club that I couldn't have done on my own. I just wasn't shown the right ways, tools, tips, or tricks as a young kid, so I thought that was the only way — because it was all I knew. In saying that, I did have some amazing times, and I wouldn't change anything.

How did it benefit your life?

Nothing in the club really benefited my life, looking back on it — I could have done all the same things without it.

How did it hinder your life?

It hindered my life because I missed out on so many important family events, friends' events, and things that were super important to me. Looking back now, I deeply regret how many times I said no to people who genuinely loved and cared for me, and who are still in my life.

Do you have any standout stories or experiences?

Definitely the national runs — they were the biggest parties of the year. All the clubs got together, all the chapters came together, and we partied from clubhouse to clubhouse, pub to pub. Lots of strippers, drugs, and alcohol.

These were the best times of the year because everyone came together. You might not have seen some of the boys for years — maybe they'd been in jail, stuck on bail or parole, or just tied down with work or family. But at the runs, everyone showed up.

Is there really a brotherhood or code of loyalty?

I think there is a brotherhood in clubs and gangs. But it can be misinterpreted, and sometimes money or ego gets put before loyalty and brotherhood — myself included. I've done things I'm not proud of and deeply regret. I've done things to people I can't take back, but I do regret them.

What would you say to people wishing to join a bike club for the first time?

I'd ask them to really think about what freedom means to them. Because once your freedom is taken away, there is no brotherhood. The boys aren't there to back you up, the drugs and money aren't there, and the gangs aren't there to protect you. You're one out, in a jail cell.

Most of the time, the visits drop off. Sometimes you don't get visits. Sometimes the boys don't send you money. The only people you really have are your family — and you become a burden on them.

So think about what you want to get out of a club, what your purpose is in joining, and then weigh that against going to jail.

How was your life initially after leaving a bike club, and how did you get out?

When I first left the club, it was very hard. I was lonely, taking a lot of drugs, and worried about all the people I had wronged. I was paranoid about the cops kicking in my door. It was the hardest time, because I didn't have much of a support network — my whole crew were dealers, bikers, and gangsters.

Would you ever consider joining a club again?

No. I have too much going on now, and I love not looking over my shoulder for police or other clubs.

How is your life now after some time away from club life?

My life now is amazing — 10 out of 10. Some things are hard, and I go through busy periods, but I always remember what those big weekends looked like, coming down off drugs and alcohol, or sitting in jail in handcuffs, away from my family.

Have you ever been diagnosed with mental health issues?

Yes. I have PTSD from childhood sexual abuse. I was abused by a prison officer when I was 17, just before I turned 18, while I was in jail.

Did you receive help for these issues during, before, or after club life?

Yes, when I left the club behind and started sharing my story. I started an organisation with the compensation money I received from suing Queensland Corrections.

My father is also a survivor — his sexual abuse happened at a local primary school. This is for anyone, any Australian who's been through any institution: boys' homes, girls' homes, foster care, youth detention centres, churches or church-run institutions, missions, reserves, community-based groups, sporting teams, Guides, Scouts, after-school care, private/public/boarding schools, group homes, foster families, or wards of the state.

Do you regret joining a bike club?

I don't regret joining, but I wouldn't do it again. I don't associate with anyone from adult life anymore. A few reach out on social media, and I still have love for them, but I'm a busy man now — studying law and running my business, *About Time for Justice*.

How do you feel being in a bike club helped mould you into the person you are today? Tell us the cool things you're doing with your life.

The club helped me develop important skills, like spotting bullshit in a room and seeing who's genuine. That skill has carried into my work now.

These days, I'm focused on:

- Running *About Time for Justice*, a support work company specialising in survivors and those affected by the criminal justice system

- Support work and support coordination

- Studying law

- Public speaking and sharing my lived experience

How did you handle losing the image and identity of being a club member?

I didn't really struggle with it. I jumped straight into bettering myself and creating a personal brand.

Now I have a YouTube and Spotify channel, *Gangs, Jail, Gangs and Justice*, and I use social media to share my story:

- Facebook – Jacob Little

- Instagram – @jacob_little

- TikTok – @jacob_little

- Snapchat – jacob_little

Is it really like *Sons of Anarchy*? Any misconceptions or truths?

Some parts are true, like the partying, but most of it is bullshit. I don't mind the show, but I haven't watched the whole series. It's wildly inaccurate.

Is there anything you'd like to add, elaborate on, or summarise?

If you ever want to reach out to me to ask questions, I'm open to collaboration. I value lived experience — without us sharing our stories, we can't reach the people we need to help, the ones still stuck in that life. Every day out of jail is a new opportunity.

THE OFFICEBEARER

Aiden - age 34

What prompted you to join a motorcycle club? What bike did you ride?

My best friend was hanging around the club when I got my license, and I naturally gravitated toward it. I found the lifestyle resonated deeply with the life I was already living — the chaos, the freedom — and with the Club came the Brotherhood. Over the years, I rode a few Harleys, from Street 500s to V-Rods.

What was your experience in a 1% motorcycle club like? Were you only in the one club?

Equal parts turbulent and exhilarating. It was a lifestyle of constant motion, whether it was riding with my Brothers, clubhouse visits, or the parties we threw. There was a strong sense of camaraderie, and my Chapter truly felt like a family. I was in a Club.

How did the experience shape who you are now?

The Club life made me stronger and more resilient, but it also opened my eyes to systemic failings and societal prejudice. I learned the harsh realities of how the world operates and how judgment can follow you long after you've changed. The 1%er mentality — to face life head-on and do what needs to be done — still aligns with me today. I still channel it into every aspect of my life.

Do you think your childhood or certain events in your upbringing led you to join a club?

Absolutely. Growing up with alcoholic parents, I had an emotionally unavailable father and a controlling, anxious mother. That left me with no stability or belonging. I battled addiction myself and saw a lot of violence, which desensitised me to chaos. Joining the Club didn't seem like such a wild choice — in my eyes, it wasn't so different from any other faction of society, just more overtly raw and unfiltered.

What do you think you got out of being in a motorcycle club that you were missing in your own life?

It gave me acceptance, loyalty, and a sense of being part of something greater than myself. The Brotherhood filled a void that my personal struggles had left behind.

How did it benefit your life?

It gave me confidence, purpose, and unforgettable experiences. Riding in a pack with my Brothers remains one of my fondest memories. Something that doesn't get talked about enough — the Club's accountability helped keep me away from the hard drugs that had consumed my life before joining.

How did it hinder your life?

The stigma of being in a Club follows you, even after you've left. It's been weaponised against me in painful ways: labelling me as unstable, an addict, inherently violent, and questioning my fitness as a father. The time and commitment required by the Club also took away from other areas of my life, including my career, relationships, and personal growth.

Do you have any standout stories or experiences you would like to tell and expand on?

One fond memory is being on a Poker Run — a point-to-point event where everyone pulls a card at every stop, and whoever has the best hand at the end of the day wins.

I saw one Brother who wasn't ready, but we were already underway in a pack, riding in formation by rank. A couple of minutes on, I saw the same Brother in my mirrors get airborne over a roundabout, then swiftly pull into formation with a lit smoke in his mouth, buckling his helmet like it was nothing.

Is there truly a Brotherhood or code of loyalty?

To some, yes. For those people, the loyalty is still there today. But for many, it's conditional and confined to the Club. I've experienced both deep loyalty and heartbreaking betrayal from members — even after I left.

What would you say to someone who is considering joining a bike club for the first time?

It's a life of commitment. The Brotherhood, the thrill, the sense of purpose are undeniably there, but it will change your life in ways — for both better and worse — that you might not anticipate. It's not a decision you should make lightly.

How was your life initially after leaving a bike club?

Leaving the Club was one of the hardest decisions I've ever made. I wanted to devote my life to being a father. But there was a lot of loss in that — I lost the majority of those I was close to, I lost a lot of my identity, and I was left with emptiness despite how much joy fatherhood brought me.

Would you ever consider joining a club again?

I think it's a fantasy that will never go away. I think I'll always want to. But I don't know if I ever could.

How is your life now after some time away from club life?

Today, I utilise my lived experience in the Mental Health field — both professionally and in charity — to help others facing adversities that I've been through. I have two beautiful children and a close circle of people around me that I wouldn't be here without. I'm incredibly grateful for the life I have now.

Current life focus:

- Mental health profession and charity work
- Fatherhood
- Building a strong, supportive inner circle

Have you ever been diagnosed with mental health issues? If so, can you elaborate?

I've been diagnosed with depression, anxiety, ADHD, autism, and significant trauma. I still struggle to this day, but I now have a much better skillset to handle it.

Did you receive help for these issues during, before, or after club life?

I never really thought about this until now, but I never sought psychological help during my time in the Club. Before and after, though, yes — significantly. I think during my time in the Club, I detached from myself, and my life became about the Club.

Do you regret joining a bike club?

A lot of my time in the Club was positive, though there were negatives as well. I value what I learned from it immensely. It has caused challenges since leaving, but I still don't regret it.

Do you still see anyone from your bike club days?

I see a handful of ex-members and one current member. I still consider these people my Brothers.

How do you feel being in a bike club helped mould you into the person you are today?

The experiences I had and the lessons I learned are now a foundation I draw from. It solidified part of my identity and gave me confidence in facing life's challenges.

How did you handle getting the image/fame/identity of being a club member and then losing it again?

The greatest struggle was losing a part of my identity. I align a lot with the 1%er mentality, and finding a community that embodied it was fulfilling and missing in much of society. Losing it left a void, but it also pushed me to find new ways to live with purpose.

Is it really like *Sons of Anarchy*? Any misconceptions or truths you would like to discuss?

Sons of Anarchy is a dramatisation of that life. If you look at it from that perspective, then it is. What you see in one episode of *Sons of Anarchy* is more like a story that would be told over the bar across years or decades.

Is there anything you would like to finish, add, elaborate on, or summarise?

No comment (if you know, you know).

CHAPTER ELEVEN

THE MEMBER

("Derek")

What prompted you to join a motorcycle club? What bike did you ride?

I'd been around it since I was a young bloke, spending 16th birthdays at a local clubhouse — a good mate's old boy was president there at the time. Moving through 17–18, a lot of our friend group were recruited or looked after by different clubs. They were in a recruitment drive, and we had a reputation for being the type of blokes they wanted. At the last minute, I decided against it because my ex at the time wouldn't have a bar of it.

Throughout adulthood, I've been on all sorts of Harleys, worked closely with a couple of blokes, and still had close childhood mates in clubs that I often rode with. I always declined offers as I had too much shit going on to commit.

It wasn't until I moved to a different area, was single, and the timing just felt right. It seemed to all align too perfectly. Living regional, I joined a small chapter (since closed) of one of the world's biggest clubs, which a few close mates had already been part of for years back in my hometown. I agreed with the rules and ideologies. At the time, I was on a 2014 Breakout.

What was your experience in a 1% motorcycle club like? Were you only in the one club?

I only committed to the one club. For me, it wasn't about wanting to be a bikie; it was about wanting to be a member of *that* club. The values and what they sold me aligned with what I was looking for.

My time had so many variables — there's always good and bad. I started off in a small regional chapter with plans for expansion into other parts of the region. When things went south, I had to decide: finish up or relocate. I chose to relocate.

City life was night and day compared to what we were used to. I had some of the best times of my life, doing more in a weekend than some people would in their entire lives. But I also had some of the worst.

How did the experience shape who you are now?

It reshaped me to be a better version of myself. It taught me I'm not bulletproof, that everything has a price, and to keep my cards close to my chest. It taught me to value what I have and who I am as an individual.

Do you think your childhood or certain events in your upbringing led you to join a club?

I got gaslit into thinking I had a good childhood. We had what we needed — the oldies worked hard — but they never had much time for us, and we weren't a very emotionally tender family. I always struggled to fit in with people who had good relationships with their parents.

I played up a fuck tonne when I was younger, always in and out of home, in trouble with the cops, even sent across the country at one point because I was too difficult. Always copping hidings until I was too big to be pushed around anymore.

My teenage years were full of drugs, violence, petty theft, and constant police harassment. I've been surrounded by crims for as long as I can remember.

What led me to eventually join was that I'd turned my life around. I moved away and was doing well in my profession. But I was surrounded by people who'd never done anything wrong, and I couldn't relate. Sharing stories, I'd get treated like a crook. My past haunted me, and I just never really fit in.

What did you get out of being in a motorcycle club that you were missing in your own life?

Belonging and acceptance. In the club, it didn't matter if you were the baddest cunt on earth or had never had a speeding ticket. It was about who you were as a person, not your past.

How did it benefit your life?

It showed me the path I was meant to be on, or at least guided me to one that felt right.

It gave me the freedom to be unapologetically myself, not pretending I hadn't lived the life I had.

I had unforgettable experiences — travelling the country, even the world, to see brothers. Made a tonne of money moving what I was putting up my nose, women hanging off me, and riding every day.

How did it hinder your life?

We went to war at one point. Life was hectic: couldn't be alone, guarding assets, clubhouses, even members' homes. Constantly looking over my shoulder. Banned from riding because it was so unsafe. Shootings, bashings — nothing was off limits. It traumatised the fuck out of my missus at the time.

My professional life took a hit. I threw it in to be a full-time bikie. That also meant being a full-time drug dealer, which didn't pair well with a nose for coke. I was off my head every day, smashing lines before getting on the Harley, tearing through peak-hour traffic, headphones in, riding on the edge.

I also fucked my relationship. Well, I fucked it with my choices.

Do you have any standout stories or experiences?

One stands out: sitting at mine with the vice president and a couple of mates on a Friday night. Out of nowhere, he asked if I was coming across the country the next day for an event. I said I couldn't be fucked, had bills and lawyers. He said, "Fuck it, I'll pay for ya." We booked flights at midnight, on a plane four hours later. Banned from the casino for suspected money laundering, we checked into another hotel instead. A big bag of rack waiting for us. Partied until the event, supported a brother, then on to a strip club with 30 of us, 10 girls, and a private bar. Partied all the way to the airport, home within 24 hours — a week's worth crammed into half a weekend.

Another: the last national run. Coming into Melbourne, nearly 300 bikes strong, police chopper overhead, cars front and back, completely owning the road. Music blaring. The presence demanded respect — or fear. That feeling was insane.

Is there truly a Brotherhood or code of loyalty?

From my experience, yes and no. The national and international brotherhood was killer — blokes who didn't know you treated you like family.

But not in my chapter. We preached it, but there was a purple circle. Once you made it into that, you were fucked if they wanted you out.

What would you say to someone who is considering joining a bike club for the first time?

Write your own story. You'll hear a thousand reasons not to and a thousand reasons to do it. Everyone's experience is different.

Someone once said in a meeting: *"We're bikies, not Boy Scouts."* Pretty self-explanatory. Weigh up your options.

Learn quickly what's club and what's personal. If it's personal, make sure you're getting paid — people will take advantage.

How was your life initially after leaving a bike club, and how did you get out?

Life was brutal. I lost everything that mattered in a week and a half.

It was a long process. My fiancée hated the Club, gave me the "me or the club" speech. I told her she couldn't ask me to choose. The prez wasn't happy, tried driving a wedge between us. She eventually took her ring off, and that was my turning point. I started saying no more often, but when the prez found out, he lost it.

Eventually, after a brutal attack from him, I was booted. Harley gone, things collected, followed home. That was the end of it.

Would you ever consider joining a club again?

I've been approached, told "it's different here," but I'm not over what happened. Happy for a beer, clubhouse visit, or ride, but I'm not ready to wear colours again.

How is your life now after some time away from club life?

Life's not much different to before my last chapter. Back in my profession and smashing it. But I've still got a reputation. People either want to buy me a beer or fight me. No middle ground.

I'm more diplomatic now — bail conditions force me to be. But lay hands on me and you'll be dealt with.

Have you ever been diagnosed with mental health issues?

As a young bloke, I was diagnosed manic depressive around 12–13, with anxiety, eating and sleeping disorders, plus drug and alcohol addiction in my later teens.

Recently, I've been professionally diagnosed with:

- Depression
- Anxiety disorder
- Bipolar disorder
- Complex PTSD
- ADHD

Did you receive help for these issues during, before, or after club life?

I got some help as a kid, but hated it. Through my teens and early adulthood, I self-medicated with drugs.

Since leaving, I've sorted my shit more naturally. If it gets too much, I'll take the doctor's advice on meds.

Do you regret joining a bike club?

Nah. Can't regret your life.

I am remorseful for things I did, but I don't regret joining.

Do you still see anyone from your bike club days?

Yes, a few. Some I'll be mates with forever. But I keep boundaries now — I don't want to know certain things.

How do you feel being in a bike club helped mould you into the person you are today? Tell us the cool things you're doing with your life.

It taught me that a man doesn't have to be violent, but he must be capable of it. Taught me to play things closer to my chest and trust my gut.

These days, I'm:

- Back to working in my profession

- Helping a mate build a business from the ground up — now with heavy vehicles, a yard, and a six-man crew

- Travelling across five states and 30 mine sites this year

- Looking at starting a group for blokes like me — not just bikies, but anyone trying to adapt to new lives after running hard in their past.

How did you handle losing the image/identity of being a club member?

Didn't change me much. Always had a big personality. People who didn't know me still assume I'm in.

Is it really like *Sons of Anarchy*?

Never watched a single episode. Used to joke: *"I love that life, why would I watch people pretend to?"*

Anything you'd like to finish with?

Since leaving the club, losing the missus, and starting life over, I've struggled with identity, goals, health, and letting people in. The only person I've managed to let close is a screw (prison officer) I met on Tinder — now one of the best humans in my life.

Don't let past stigmas ruin your future. Treat people the way you want to be treated. And if you need help — get it. Ask a mate, a colleague, or a doctor.

At the time of writing this, I'm still struggling like fuck — almost took my life a few days ago. But it can only get better. One day at a fucking time boys.

CHAPTER TWELVE

THE MEMBER (SHORT AND SWEET)

(Anonymous)

What prompted you to join a motorcycle club? What bike did you ride?

Joined because of the brotherhood — you do anything for each other. Rode a 2012 Wide Glide (103 ci).

What was your experience in a 1% motorcycle club like? Were you only in the one club?

It was good at the start, until cracks formed. Only one club.

How did the experience shape who you are now?

It's made me keep my circle even smaller.

Do you think your childhood or certain events in your upbringing led you to join a club?

Nah — had a good upbringing.

What do you think you got out of being in a motorcycle club that you were missing in your own life?

Identity. Everyone knew not to fuck around with me.

How did it benefit your life?

Gave me reasons to stay close with club members.

How did it hinder your life?

Took up too much time — sometimes three to four days a week. I missed family events, birthdays, etc.

Do you have any standout stories or experiences you would like to tell and expand on?

Nah. My issues were a group of close friends nomming up and coming into a chapter where old members wouldn't accept change.

Is there really a brotherhood or code/loyalty?

100% — there is.

What would you say to people wishing to join a bike club for the first time?

Unless you're single and plan on staying single, don't. It's a shit life — always looking over your shoulder.

How was your life initially after leaving a bike club and how did you get out?

My wife got cancer; it was my escape route. We had a meeting and I handed my colours in on the table with everyone present in the chapter.

Would you ever consider joining a club again?

Never. I don't even ride to say the temptation. Four old members passed away from bike accidents in the last year.

How is your life now after some time away from club life?

110% better. No stress, no drama. Quality family time. Closer with my wife. My business runs better.

Have you ever been diagnosed with mental health issues? And if so, can you elaborate?

No.

Did you receive help for these pre-, during, or post-club life issues?

No.

Do you regret joining a bike club?

Yes.

Do you still see anyone from your bike club days?

Yes — quite a few.

How do you feel being in a bike club helped mould you into the person you are today? Tell us the cool things you're doing with your life.

100% made me keep quality over quantity in friends.

How did you handle getting the image/fame/identity of being a club member and then losing it again?

Just keep busy with family and hobbies.

Is it really like *Sons of Anarchy*? Any misconceptions or truths you would like to discuss?

Yes — my wife and I are watching it now. Lots of it does relate.

Anything you would like to finish, add, elaborate, or summarise with?

No — all good.

CHAPTER THIRTEEN

FULL MEMBER

(St. Pat) joined an MC before stepping up and is now 33

What prompted you to join a motorcycle club?

I wanted to ride with a bunch of people who ride regularly, and I wanted the solidarity/brotherhood. I didn't have heaps of friends growing up and was bullied a bit in primary school. So I guess it's a bit of a no-brainer what attracted me.

What bike did you ride?

2012 Street Bob / 2008 Night Rod Special.

What was your experience in a 1% motorcycle club like? Were you only in the one club?

Overall, it was a very exhilarating, insightful, stressful, chaotic, and fun seven years of my life.

I was only in one club. I went to a few car and bike shows of multiple clubs, did a bit of scouting, and after a funny head-fuck of an interaction with a full patch member at a bike show, I chose the one I thought was gonna be *The One*. Lol.

How did the experience shape who you are now?

By being exposed to and seeing people operate in many types of situations that were described to me at the time as a "necessary evil." It gives you a very different perspective on how some humans justify their wrongdoings. From petty grievances to life-changing altercations, it's definitely made me more rigid with trust.

Do you think your childhood or certain events in your upbringing led you to join a club?

Yes.

What did you get out of being in a motorcycle club that you were missing in your own life?

Friends. I wasn't raised on the fundamentals of "Brotherhood" but more so "Friendship," so the term brotherhood was fairly new to me.

When I say friends, I mean actual mates — the ones who'd buy you a Happy Meal if you were short a few bucks because you lashed out your cash aaaalllll the time to make sure everyone was having a good time. I just wanted decent people in my life who'd have my back and go on rides with me, not just take advantage of me. Lol — how wrong I was. (Don't get me wrong, it wasn't all bad.)

How did it benefit your life?

It taught me to be more confident in myself.

One member in particular, who'd had a very colourful life, taught me many valuable lessons. One of my favourites was the old Bob Hudson classic *The Newcastle Song* — just sat and listened at the bar after a long few days.

How did it hinder your life?

The fucking police harassment. My god, fellas, I know you gotta job to do, but far-ha-huk'n hell. The rate at which I was getting pulled over for a licence check was just a waste of taxpayers' money.

(Side note to officers who may be reading this, thinking it's dreadful and a painful process for holding us up: we actually don't care. It's in OUR job description to not hold or be in possession of prohibited substances or items in club colours, or do anything that may attract unwanted attention by law enforcement. So, for the very few convictions you actually get compared to the number of initial stops, it's fucking laughable. What seems like serious business to you, Robo-Cop is just a fun game of cat and mouse to them.)

Do you have any standout stories or experiences you would like to expand on?

Yeah. I was at a party once and a close brother said to me, "Hey, you see Brother A over there? He fuckin' hates Brother B just there, and will probably warn you about him."

"Why?" I asked. Both brothers were life members.

"Because a long time ago, Brother C (not at this party for soon-to-be obvious reasons) ratted on some brothers. Some brothers were locked up for what they did. As retaliation for cooperating with the police, Brother B and some accomplices found where Brother C was. They tied him and his partner up and started to gang rape her whilst they made Brother C watch. During this, Brother B made himself comfortable in the house and proceeded to make himself a sandwich and eat it whilst he watched."

I don't think Brother A liked mistreating women.

Is there really a Brotherhood or code/loyalty?

Yes, but it is divided into different groups. Whether the chapter as a whole has it, or groups of members from different chapters creating their own inner circles, you'll find it.

What would you say to people wishing to join a bike club for the first time?

Read the new book. (No comment.) The guide for prospects and probates.

How was your life initially after leaving a bike club?

Confusing at the start, filling in the blanks, and then a bit of fear of repercussions.

But a good brother once told me:

>*"What you do whilst in this club will follow you out."*

I'm sure you've seen on the news ex-members leaving — being shot to death or meeting some sort of grisly end. It happens more frequently than you'd realise, just on a smaller scale. Whether it be bashings, taking bikes, or plain old standover tactics.

I was fortunate enough to lead a pretty good club life, though I did have a few grievances that kept me in what feels like a mental prison for a few years after I left. I made amends where necessary and realised it was a lot of self-forgiveness. I also looked forward to a good new positive life, helping others and giving back to the community.

Would you ever consider joining a club again?

Not unless it's my own. Hahahahaha.

How is your life now after some time away from club life?

Peaceful.

Yeah sure, it sounds like it's all fun and games — wearing what you think is the coolest, most badass muthafuckin' patch above all other clubs, riding some Harley clapedy-clap-clap ma-bob, cruising down whatever road tickles your goat, bitches starin', blokes gawkin', random old bloke wavin' g'day like he knows ya. Fuck yeah, sick, look at me, this is grouse...

Then reality sets in. You gotta keep in mind that a bro was shot last week and is still in the hospital. Looks like it's a random thing aimed at the club, and you could be next. Undercover police are also running brothers off the road.

Have you ever been diagnosed with mental health issues? If so, can you elaborate?

ADHD. Can't elaborate much — I'm still in the midst of diagnosis. Mum refused to have me tested as a kid because she didn't believe in ADD or ADHD.

Did you receive help for these issues during, before, or after club life?

Post.

Do you regret joining a bike club?

The answer changes every day, for so many reasons — some good, some bad.

Do you still see anyone from your bike club days?

Yeah, every now and then, I touch base with other ex-members who saw the light and chose the right, better route. Those who are still tied up in the life I haven't really got the time of day for, unless they genuinely want to leave.

How do you feel being in a bike club helped mould you into the person you are today?

It helped me detect bullshit even better. Once you see how some of these members do business, you see it on a smaller scale in the outside world — just in a more polite manner where people are a bit timid to call it out.

How did you handle getting the image/fame/identity of being a club member and then losing it again?

It's all ego and street cred at the end of the day. For me, I mentally checked out a long time before my exodus.

If you know what an "ego death" is, this is where you will achieve this milestone; if you don't, Google it.

For me, my ego had already died months prior. It was, as I've mentioned earlier, about coming to terms with any wrongdoings I may have done during my time in the club.

Is it really like *Sons of Anarchy*? Any misconceptions or truths you'd like to discuss?

Absolutely. *Sons of Anarchy* just happens in a much quicker and condensed time frame for visual stimulation.

Brothers run underground brothels, criminals are shooting at people, kidnappings, torture, rape, extortion, houses getting run through, police raids, public executions, and severed heads. It's all happened.

Is there anything you would like to finish, add, elaborate on, or summarise?

Any active 1%er who took part in the COVID-19 vaccination program... You failed! You coward! Weak c*#t! Worthless shell of a man! You betrayed what it means to be a true 1%er. You betrayed your brothers, present and lost — but worst of all, you betrayed yourself.

To hear, *"but I was gonna lose my business/car,"* is a cop-out to the brothers who refused the Government-mandated vaccine and lost what they had, or had to adapt a new way of living.

Any active 1%er with a Covid jab should hand in their vest.

A 1%er is 1% of a hundred of us who have given up on society and the politicians' one-way law.

That was the perfect moment in history for 1%ers to stand together in solidarity against not only the mandates and restrictions. It's funny you can organise a weekend-long AGM (National Run) with catering, hotel bookings, entertainment, plan ride routes, liaise with police, and the list goes on, but you can't organise to protect what you say is your way of living.

I think it definitely says a lot about what is going to happen to motorcycle clubs as a whole. It would seem they'd rather spend money on keeping the party going than spending the money to keep the club going.

A MOTHER'S PERSPECTIVE

(Anonymous Mum)

Did you know anything about motorcycle clubs before your son joined? Did you have experience with them prior?

I did have some knowledge, as my three brothers were friends with members from different clubs. I sometimes went along with them to open fundraiser days/nights.

I found these events to be open and friendly and never felt unsafe. But in saying that, you were told of areas you could not go — this is where business was being done.

What was your opinion of motorcycle clubs?

Back when I was young, I found them exciting and scary at the same time. I was aware of the seediness, but because of my brothers' association with them, I felt safe.

I remember drinking at a coastal hotel with friends when a large group of bikers rode into the carport. My friends got very nervous and wanted to leave. A member came up to me and said, "You're so-and-so's sister, you're ok." At the time, I thought that was pretty cool. We chatted with them and then left, but the next day I heard the pub was closed because they had trashed it.

My younger brother was also an associate of some club members until a case of mistaken identity with new members left him with a broken jaw, concussion, broken ribs, and a broken leg. They were reprimanded, but the damage was done. I decided then that clubs weren't exciting — they could be dangerous.

What were your thoughts about your son joining a club?

I was immediately scared for him — that it would change who he was, close a lot of doors, and alter his life. I didn't like that he was joining a club.

He knew this and tried to convince me: "It's not like you think, it's a brotherhood, and you don't have to do anything you don't want to."

I knew he was searching for an identity. Being raised in a house of women after I divorced his father, this offered him brothers, male companionship, and family — or so he thought. I knew he had made up his mind, so I decided to stay close, support, and watch, rather than alienate him.

Do you think certain childhood events and experiences early on led him to be attracted to that lifestyle?

Yes, definitely. Growing up in a low socio-economic, female-dominated household was hard for him. I was struggling with a marriage breakdown, which brought back anxiety and low self-esteem from abuse I'd experienced when I was young, as well as the stress of raising two young children alone.

I didn't see how this was affecting him. I put him into martial arts and army cadets. As he got older, he formed a car club, then a non-patch motorcycle club, and from this, he eventually joined a patched club.

What do you think he got out of the motorcycle club world?

At first, he did get the brotherhood and family as promised. But as time went on it changed — drugs, partying, toxic relationships.

He did get life experience. He saw people with drug addiction, mental health problems, and alcohol issues. I remember calling them the "lost boys" — all had some form of trauma, mental health issue, or substance abuse problem. Later on, he started trying to help them, which eventually led him to leave the club and start his mental health business. In that way, yes — it brought him to where he is today.

Do you think it hindered his life? If so, why?

Yes, definitely. Drugs, partying, toxic relationships. Ninety-five per cent of your time and identity is demanded by the club.

He lost friends who didn't want to be part of his life while he was in the club, though some have come back since. There wasn't much time for friendships outside of the club — sometimes not much time for family either.

There are other consequences: no gun licence, no government jobs, lots of closed doors. Choosing this lifestyle has consequences.

Do you have any standout stories or experiences — things that happened to you or to him, good or bad?

I do. While he was in the club, I sometimes woke to late-night messages from toxic female partners of members, telling me he was where he should be, the happiest he'd ever been. That wasn't true — he was partying and in a toxic relationship.

We did go to a couple of open fundraiser nights as he asked us. All the members there were friendly and treated me with respect.

Do you really think they are a brotherhood, with a code and loyalty?

I feel it starts out that way in a new member's eyes. They're recruited from non-patch clubs and fed this ideology.

The club motto is: *What happens in the club, stays in the club.* Loyalty to the club is definitely there. But not always with each other — it depends on circumstances. When you leave the club, the brotherhood ends.

What would you say to other parents whose sons are joining a club?

Talk to them openly and objectively. Keep communication lines open. Stay in contact visually. Chances are they'll have already made their decision. Take the journey with them — set boundaries, but be ready to support and guide where you can.

Did you attend any club functions or events?

Yes. At the first one, I felt a bit set up. I was invited to an open night. Everyone was friendly and chatty. Then he came over and told me straight out that he was nomming and joining the club.

I didn't know what to say or how to respond. I felt numb. I had to decide on the spot how to handle it. If I got angry or tried to talk him out of it, I would have alienated him. So I decided to stay close and support him, as he had already made his decision.

Were there certain fears, worries, or concerns about him being in a club? How did you handle that?

Yes — many. I feared for his mental health, with the partying and drugs. I worried constantly for his safety.

He spent 95% of his time with club members. I honestly didn't see the partying, or I would've gone nuts. But I saw the behaviour changes — toxic relationships, personality shifts. He wasn't the same, even with us.

How is his life now after some time away from the club lifestyle?

His life is totally different. He's kicking goals, has a lovely wife, and has built a mental health business from the ground up.

He's an inspirational man today. I'm very proud of who he has become.

Have you ever been diagnosed with mental health issues?

I had trauma from childhood sexual abuse, which I buried for a long time. It manifested into behaviour I thought was normal — I couldn't show emotions, kept everything inside when stressed, sad, or angry.

I was raised to keep emotions in check and be strong. But it came to a head when my son had his breakdown and confessed he was seeing a psychologist. When I couldn't respond how I should have, I made an appointment myself. Best thing I ever did.

After many sessions, EMDR, homework, and strategies, I was able to let my family know why I had been emotionally rigid.

I handle it now with acceptance, strategies, and occasional online support.

Did parts of his club life ever leave you feeling relieved?

No, not until he started studying and slowly got on the path to leaving the club.

Going back, if you could have stopped him from joining or given advice before joining, what would it be?

I would've been stronger about expressing my concerns and fears, and asked him not to — even though I knew he would anyway.

Can you give an outside perspective on what you think about the club? Was there drama, hierarchy, how were the women, and "old ladies" associated with the club?

The club is cultish — it becomes their family while making workers out of them.

Most of the women drawn to the members are toxic, with drug and substance abuse issues. This makes for toxic relationships. They pretend to support each other, but really, they just want to party.

Noming is entry-level. Then a patch is earned. Roles include vice president, sergeant-at-arms, president, and nomads. The women did not attend meetings but held status depending on who their partner was.

How do you feel being in the bike club environment helped mould him into the person he is today?

Life experience. You need strength of character, morals, and ethics going into a club to come out whole.. He had this. The things he saw, did, and was challenged by moulded him, showed him the man he wanted to be — and the man he didn't.

Do you think the image/identity of it all changed him? If so, how?

You can't live a club lifestyle and not be changed.

He went in looking for a brotherhood but saw how drugs, toxic relationships, mental health deterioration, and trauma affected members. The club becomes your identity.

He was deeply affected by it, but now he's strong, setting goals, and kicking them.

Is it really like *Sons of Anarchy*? Any misconceptions or truths?

Not that I witnessed. The best way I can explain it: it's like a cult. They send out soldiers to recruit, to work, and eventually to do business to make big money.

The idea of brotherhood is a misconception. You leave, and the brotherhood is finished.

Some clubs are very bad — violence, drug dealing, debt collecting, prostitution. They all do business, but some are worse than others. Turf wars definitely exist, and consequences for theft can be severe.

Anything you'd like to add, finish, or summarise with?

When members leave a club, a part of them will miss parts of that life. They'll feel loneliness and grief. They'll need a lot of support in the transition and a new sense of belonging. It's out there — just reach out.

CHAPTER FIFTEEN

THE EX-MEMBER

(Nick Wickham) - 34

What prompted you to join a motorcycle club? What bike did you ride?

I started hanging around the bike scene when I was struggling with mental health issues and difficult circumstances. I found belonging and value with the people there — a support network of like-minded riders — combined with my love of motorcycles.

I started out on dirt bikes at 13 and got my licence at 22 with a Yamaha V-Star Custom. That bike was therapy — freedom, adrenaline, an escape. My uncle let me ride his Harley Night Train one day, and the moment I hit the throttle I was hooked. Soon after, I financed a Harley Iron 883, then traded up to a Harley Street Bob — my all-time favourite bike.

What was your experience in a 1% motorcycle club like? Were you only in one club?

Mixed. The positives: camaraderie, brotherhood, support, wild parties, long rides, and hilarious memories. The clubhouse felt like home. Brothers fed me and helped me when I was broke. The club was family.

But the negatives were real — my values were tested, and my family's safety weighed on me. I worried about raids, threats, and violence. At one point, a dangerous figure swore to shoot anyone in our colours. Eventually, leadership changes and chapter closures shifted the club's direction. My priorities became my kids and partner, and I made the painful decision to leave.

How did the experience shape who you are now?

It made me stronger, more resilient, and unwilling to accept disrespect. I discovered my loyalty, adaptability, and grit.

But I also struggled with loss of identity. I became hypervigilant, always scanning my surroundings, conditioned to expect conflict. That sense of readiness still lingers.

Do you think your childhood or certain events in your upbringing led you to join a club?

Yes. My parents worked hard but were often absent — Mum working, Dad a truck driver. I craved stability and father figures, which I found in older members.

I was bullied extensively as a kid, leaving deep scars on my self-worth. Being in a respected (sometimes feared) group felt like regaining worth. The club filled that void — but it also fed my co-dependency, relying on external validation instead of finding it within.

What did you get out of being in a motorcycle club that you were missing?

Worthiness of love, support, and attention.

How did it benefit your life?

It kept me afloat when I needed belonging most. Without it, I might have turned to substance abuse or other unhealthy groups.

How did it hinder your life?

Leaving ripped away my identity. The lifestyle consumed me, and when it was gone, I had to rebuild from scratch. It was foreign and painful.

Do you have any standout stories?

None I'm comfortable sharing. Some things are best left unsaid.

Is there really a Brotherhood or code/loyalty?

Yes and no. The code was enforced — even presidents were expelled for breaking rules. Loyalty existed, but often conditional. Brotherhood was genuine for some, superficial for others.

What would you say to people wishing to join a bike club?

Ask yourself:

- Will my life be the same in 10 years?

- Do I want a family or a career that conflicts with club life?

- Am I filling a void?

- Can I handle police harassment, raids, violence, and strained relationships?

- Am I ready for the costs and commitment?

Don't rush it. Understand the whole picture.

How was your life after leaving a club? How did you get out?

Miserable and relieved. I lost my identity and my bike, but I gained freedom from conflict, politics, and danger. I had more time for my children and for peace.

I left on good terms — handing over everything properly, including my Harley and clubhouse key. The club understood, even if they weren't happy.

Would you consider joining again?

Never. If I wanted back in, I wouldn't have left.

How is life now after time away from club life?

Peaceful. I miss some aspects, but I no longer romanticise them. My energy goes to my kids, goals, and personal growth.

Current life focus:

- Buying my first property

- Training at an MMA gym (working toward mentoring/leadership)

- Prioritising mental health and self-work
- Setting and achieving personal goals

Have you ever been diagnosed with mental health issues?

Yes:

- ADHD (recent, now medicated)
- Anxiety
- Anxious attachment style

Medication and self-reflection have improved my emotional regulation and self-understanding.

Did you receive help before, during, or after club life?

Post. Only recently have I truly confronted my issues, managed triggers, and learned to be secure.

Do you regret joining?

Yes — because my reasons for joining weren't healthy.

Do you still see anyone from your club days?

Yes, some ex-members. No current members.

How did being in a club mould you? What are you doing with your life now?

I don't credit the club. Who I am today is from my own work, time, and determination.

Now I'm:

- Writing for this book to help others
- Planning property ownership

- Building a healthy outlet through MMA
- Stronger mentally than ever before

How did you handle the image/identity of being a member and then losing it?

I never joined for image or notoriety. Wearing the patch was pride in brotherhood, not ego. Losing it didn't affect me because I wasn't in it for fame.

Is it really like *Sons of Anarchy*?

Yes and no. Everything in the show happened — shootings, explosions, raids — but not at the frequency they portray.

The biggest difference: clubs don't sit down and plan crimes together. Real meetings were about who embarrassed themselves drunk, organising runs, or whose turn it was to clean the clubhouse.

Anything you'd like to add?

Whatever major life decision you face — joining a club or otherwise — make it as the most healed version of yourself, with clarity and full understanding of what it means for you and your life.

FROM STREET GANG TO CLUB

What prompted you to join a motorcycle club? What bike did you ride?

My story goes all the way back to childhood. Looking at the "mini lives" I've lived — different phases and groups — the pattern was always belonging, connection, community, and purpose.

I grew up in Melbourne's western suburbs, almost living in two worlds. At home, my old man ruled with an iron fist. He called himself "the iron fist in a velvet glove" — smooth on the outside, savage on the inside. He hated swearing, laziness, and "no-hopers," and would smash our heads for chewing wrong or using poor vocabulary.

Meanwhile, the suburb changed into a ghetto of commission houses, street gangs, and drugs. At home, I was pushed to be a winner. Outside, I lived among the very "no-hopers" he despised.

By 14, I told him to fuck off and moved in with a known dealer. We set up houses with hydro, scored endless butterfly knives, and ran a crew that thought it ruled three train stations and half the local beach. With my brothers' reputations behind me, I felt like a king.

I dropped out of school. Life was sex, drugs, rock 'n' roll, and hip hop. Until it crashed. My best mate spiralled into heroin and armed robberies and ended up in max security. My crew fell apart. Then, just before my 21st, I went to court for nearly killing someone with a baseball bat. I knew change was needed.

I leaned into my only skill from Dad: confidence and talking. Sales were my way out. I thrived, bought a house, had kids, and moved interstate. But I never shook the taste for connection with people cut from the same cloth. Eventually, I bought a Harley (should've bought that jet ski!) and was soon tied to a top-tier 1% chapter.

What was your experience in a 1% motorcycle club like? Were you only in one club?

Like many, social club, feeder club, and then colours. I organised charity rides, hot rod shows, and rallies. I built connections across rival clubs. Hardcore men — even high-profile ones in the news — came to my garage for counsel. Somehow, I became an unofficial ear for guys who couldn't trust anyone else.

There was connection, mission, and belonging. But also toxic masculinity: compassion was weakness. "Fuck the world" meant respect. Brotherhood? Only so far. Loyalty was always to the club first. You're as likely to be bashed by your own as a rival.

Everyone had roles. Some wheeled and dealed. Some bashed. My "specialty" was sex — I was the go-to guy for hookups across the city. People saw me as someone who brought relief, not stress.

How did the experience shape who you are now?

It consumed me. I neglected family, health, and work. I spiralled — drinking slabs of Jack, drowning in swingers' clubs and kink factories, self-harm, and almost admitted to psych wards. Two social workers checked on me daily to keep me alive.

I looked like I was living the dream. Inside, the lights were off. Medication turned me into a zombie. Cutting was the only thing that made me feel alive.

Eventually, I lost my house and career. But hitting rock bottom made me ask: if I won $50 million, what would I do? The answer was always: help people. That realisation set me on a new path.

Do you think your childhood led you here?

Yes. Pack mentality was in me like football clubs, poker groups, gyms, sex communities. I go all in. If I'd bought that jet ski, maybe I'd be competing in Thailand instead of riding a Harley. But growing up with gangs and poverty, the path was inevitable.

What did you get out of a club that you were missing?

It wasn't about filling a void. It was the next phase of belonging and purpose, just like every other stage of my life.

How did it benefit you? How did it hinder you?

At its peak, I felt like a king. Protected. Untouchable. Rock star life. But everything has a price. Clubs police themselves with force. That wasn't me. My internal conflict led to mental breakdown, self-destruction, and loss.

Standout memories?

Yes, brothers rallying behind each other, raising tens of thousands for charity, supporting mates in crisis. Many died — illness, crashes, overdoses, murder. I cherish the friendships more than the chaos.

Is there really a brotherhood?

It's loyalty to the club first. That can create brotherhood, but it's conditional. Some say it's as thin as patch stitching. I say it's what you make of it.

Advice to new members?

Patched membership is an accomplishment. But know this: you may one day go to jail for something you didn't do, lose your family, job, and home, and then get called out to do it all again. If that doesn't sit with you, stay the fuck away.

How was life after leaving?

I left with blessings — because I'd helped many. I threw myself into study and volunteer work. Slowly, connections dwindled. Fake friends fell away. Readjusting wasn't easy — no more walking into places with instant respect. But better that I faded than became another old cocky bloke trying to hold on.

Would you join again?

Bike clubs? Never. Sex clubs? Maybe!

Mental health?

Yes — total breakdown: self-harm, suicide attempts, months in bed. Wrong meds made it worse. Intensive outreach saved me. Purpose became my therapy. Studying social work gave me reason to live.

Regrets?

Yes and no. I'd probably own a house and earn more if I never touched a bike. Why didn't I buy that jet ski? But every step shaped who I am today — balanced, with work I love.

Do you still see people from those days?

Rarely, not in person. Some online. I still reach out when old brothers are in strife — even if I don't condone their actions.

How did the club shape you? What do you do now?

It gave me lived experience to pair with formal training. Now I help people overcome barriers, drawing on street smarts and adversity.

Losing the identity?

It took time. I'd always had notoriety, through family and later clubs. One day, you're a rock star. The next, you're grey-haired, straight, and just another worker. That adjustment was tough — but it gave me purpose.

Sons of Anarchy — truth or myth?

Some things are accurate — politics especially. But Aussie clubs vary: from old-school bogan to 90's gangster rapper vibes. Some members live crime-free, others breathe it. Not as scripted as TV, but politics are real.

Final words?

- Just say no.
- Stick with a good GP.
- Don't buy into the romance.
- If you do join, don't be a dog. Back your brothers.
- And keep condoms handy — demand is high!

CHAPTER SEVENTEEN

THE FULL MEMBER

What prompted you to join a motorcycle club? What bike did you ride?

I wanted to belong to something great. I wanted the commitment and a brotherhood who were there for me. I had a Street 500 because I was on a restricted licence.

What was your experience in a 1% motorcycle club like? Were you only in the one club?

In the beginning it was crazy — full on, and I loved it. The attention you get from the public almost makes you feel like a rock star. People say they're intimidated, but they're still there with their phones out taking photos, filming, and posting it online. Seeing that cycle back with all the comments can be a good ego boost — and a good laugh with the hate comments too.

I always said I'd stick with one club. If I left, I was done with the life.

How did the experience shape who you are now?

Prior to my experience as a 1%er, I wasn't good at sticking up for myself. But when you're wearing that patch, you need to show you aren't fearful and won't back down. These days I've calmed down, become a lot less hostile, but I still don't take shit from anyone. I just find conflict less often now.

Do you think your childhood or certain events in your upbringing led you to join a club?

I was heavily bullied all my life. I never had good friends at school and had lots of self-esteem issues — which made me the perfect candidate for being in an OMCG. A lot of my brothers had similar experiences growing up.

What did you get out of being in a motorcycle club that you were missing in your life?

At the end of the day, I did have brothers there for me anytime. The loyalty can be unreal. But at the same time, it's a lot like high school — people who don't like you for whatever reason. That's what's wrong with a lot of clubs: they fuel toxicity to boost certain egos.

How did it benefit your life?

It gave me accountability. You can't just do whatever you want — there's a chain of command. If someone along the chain says no, then it's a solid no.

How did it hinder your life?

I lost a lot of time with my family. It drained my relationship with my partner. As a full patch member, I was always doing something — it never stopped.

Do you have any standout stories or experiences?

The big misconception is that people see the bikes, jewellery, girls, and money, and assume they'll get the same. That's far from the case. You need a good income to be in a club: dues, parties, interstate flights, funerals, bike repairs, vests, and patches. Centrelink or selling a couple ounces a week won't cut it.

Is there really a Brotherhood or code/loyalty?

To an extent. Most brothers were there for me and were loyal. But I had members who didn't like me — some tried to add my partner on socials, some ganged up on me over nothing. From what I've seen, most clubs have a toxic side fuelled by egos.

What would you say to people wishing to join a bike club for the first time?

If you have kids, a wife, or already have decent friends and family, you don't need this bullshit in your life.

How was your life initially after leaving, and how did you get out?

I left on good standing. Most clubs require a dividend when it comes to leaving — they're fuelled by money, and no one leaves for free.

Would you ever consider joining a club again?

Nope, not ever again. I regret it more than anything. It wasn't worth what it caused.

How is your life now after time away from club life?

Life is so much better now:

- I get every night with my family

- No middle-of-the-night phone calls

- No leaving work in the middle of the day for club business

- I can focus on my family, my mental health, and my physical health without interference.

Have you ever been diagnosed with mental health issues?

Yes. My honest truth? Clubs are full of broken men. They've all had something traumatic happen. Anyone who says otherwise has their head up their arse.

Did you get help for these pre-, post-, or during club life?

I tried at all points. But post-club life, I can actually prioritise it.

Do you regret joining a bike club?

101%. The most gangsta thing I've ever done was leaving gang life for my family.

Do you still see anyone from your bike club days?

Yeah, from time to time, but only other ex-members.

How did being in a bike club mould you? What are you doing with your life now?

It made me more solid as a man. I'm still staunch when it comes to everyday stuff.

How did you handle losing the image/identity of being a club member?

I wanted to leave for a long time but needed to be sure. It's hard going from being seen as this big, tough person to being a civilian again. Clubs run on a military mentality — but it's a joke compared to the real thing.

Is it really like *Sons of Anarchy*?

LMAO. I hated that show. Tried to watch it but couldn't stand it. My club was nothing like it.

Anything you'd like to add?

Not everyone's experience is bad. Mine was good for the first few years — I loved it, and those are good memories. But when things go wrong in a 1%er club, they go REALLY wrong. It's stressful, overwhelming, and that's before police harassment even starts. From someone who's lived it — there are a lot better things you can do with your life.

CHAPTER EIGHTEEN

MY OWN STORY

Troy age 42

What prompted you to join a motorcycle club? What bike did you ride?

Looking back, I always knew I was going to be a member of an outlaw motorcycle club.

My uncle Colin instilled in me a love of motorcycles at a young age. I always looked up to him, and he always took me under his wing.

He actually got me my first motorbike, which I had always thought was a red scrambler. However, after writing this book and asking him, I found out it was actually an RM80, painted red.

While growing up, the majority of my friends were on farms and having either horses or motorbikes was just the thing to do. My early best friend in primary school had a KDX 250, which we affectionately called the 'green machine,' and it was the biggest junk heap I had ever seen. We spent more time fixing it than riding it, but it was a legitimate dirt bike. My cousin had a YZ 80 with white plastics and a red seat. It had a governor on it to keep us from killing ourselves with the powerband, but it was on just enough to let the powerband kick in—always at just the wrong time, every time. But again, it was a legit dirt bike.

Another one of my best friends, who probably had one of the biggest influences on my life before he passed away, was Tristian. He had a DS80, and we were both big guys. He liked nothing more than scaring the shit out of me, being on the back, drunk, going through rock fields as fast as that little bike could take us, nearly ripping our toes off hitting rocks. Bloody good times.

I begged and begged my dad to get me a bike, and he did: an old blue steel tank Kawasaki road bike with road tyres, blinkers, number plate—full-blown road spec. It even had a high and low range gear lever from memory. When I wasn't sliding it out on the potato farm ruts with everyone laughing at me, getting overtaken by my friends (laughing hysterically) in first gear without trying, while I had it pegged in top gear hunched over the tank for better aerodynamics like I was in the race of my life, I was push-starting it and having the time of my life. I smashed all the blinkers off it, ripped the number plate holder off it, blew the shocks off it, jumping the dam walls, welded them back on, and because it was quiet and had lights, I got to sneak out and go on some cheeky night rides the others could not do.

I ended up selling her to a mate to help fund a horse I was buying, and the motor ended up in a go-kart.

After a while, I realised that if I fell off a horse, it wasn't necessarily my fault, as there are two brains to worry about and a lot of time, effort and money in maintaining horses. But a dirt bike could sit there and come out whenever I wanted. Plus, my best mate (I later joined the club with) had a TT250, again white with a red seat, that he nearly got decapitated on. His dad had hung a new fence line up to keep the cows out of the back paddock, but didn't tell anyone, and my mate hit it flat out without a helmet on. His teeth ended up going through his bottom lip. Funny thing is, with the curve of a helmet, the wire would have ended up under his chin and most likely killed him. We discussed it later, while he was jokingly blowing blood bubbles out of his new holes.

His sister's boyfriend was part of a crew that rode in a style similar to the Crusty Demons and also practised martial arts. They had huge parties, and there always seemed to be hot girls around, which always helps young men make decisions. So, I got my next bike—a limited edition WR/YZ 250cc. Apparently, the story goes that they only made this for one year. It was a YZ250 2-stroke, but it had a coil pack, which meant it could be road registered—hence the WR/YZ.

This bike was terrifying. I am easily the worst rider in our group, but if we hit a straight, I had everyone. This bike was so fast that my eyes couldn't keep up with the trees going past me. Mates that raced rode this, and it would blow their socks off. I even used it for a paid job on someone's farm, rounding sheep up in a pine plantation with my best mate, and it definitely wasn't designed for that. I still miss this bike and have tried to find it again, but to no avail. When I sold it, it allowed me to spend another three months in Thailand, where I was kickboxing. So if you have this bike, please get in touch. I have very fond memories of riding it out in the country streets for a quick blast, leaving myself just enough time to sneak it back in the shed to see the police drive past.

There were other bikes in the mix, like postie bikes and a dirty old XR250, on which I learned more in one day than trying to learn on the race bike for a couple of years.

Then one day, my late brother called and asked if I was home. Half an hour later, my brother rolled up on a Virago 250, which, if you're reading this and don't know what that is, is a tiny, tiny little bike. And my brother was not a tiny, tiny little man, but the opposite, in fact. He was about 6'2", the same height as me, but weighed about 170kg. Once we got over having a laugh about that, I knew it was time to get my bike licence—even though he sold it for being too small shortly afterwards. My other best mate had just got himself a GSXR, which looked about as comfortable as sitting on a cactus, also being a big guy.

After having my licence for some time but never doing anything with it, I reconnected with some friends from my old job after coming back from Thailand. All my Asian mates had their sports bikes and WRX cars, and all my big Aussie mates had their cruisers and V8S. The differences didn't matter. At Smokos, we would always be standing around and checking out each other's bikes, sitting on each other's bikes and talking about bikes or cars. This led me to get my first official on-the-road bike, and before I even rode it, she went into the custom shop for a makeover. She was a VN Suzuki Intruder 1500cc.

This bike got so much attention that it drove Harley riders mad. There is a picture later in this book of me on a protest ride, which appeared on the news, and everyone lost their minds because they chose to feature a Suzuki Intruder in the main thumbnail. This bike was like riding a rocking chair, and it remains the most comfortable bike I've ever ridden. However, it didn't have a large fuel tank and had also been jetted and ported to give it more power, but in actual fact, it just made it more thirsty. It had less range than a Sporty, and the rear end would bounce sideways going around corners because the suspension was so low and because it was shaft-driven.

I used this bike all throughout my time as a social motorcycle president. Then, when a 1% outlaw motorcycle club asked me to become president of their new motorcycle club, I asked if I could do it on this bike, and they said yes, 100%, not a problem. Two weeks later, the president called me and said we had our AGM coming up, and the Nationals had said I needed to own either a British or an American-made bike before then.

Within a week, I had sold her and got myself a pretty cool Harley. It had an S&S motor and a few custom parts, so I was good to go—except the second time I rode it, the controls fell off in my hand and everyone said, "Welcome to the joys of having a Harley."

It didn't take me long to write this bike off. I was corner marking for a funeral, and an error was made, and long story short, I hit my cousin and then bounced off a railing on a single-car bridge, landing on top of my bike and surfed it all the way across the bridge until it stopped. But I still had momentum and used that to spring up with the bike, running the bike off the bridge. I was fairly moving when this happened, and I came away from it without a scratch—thanks to a very protective girlfriend at the time yelling at me beforehand to make sure I was wearing my safety gear, as I was walking out the door very casually dressed. We are still good friends today.

With the insurance money, we went all out fixing it and getting a custom job done. It had a 7-degree rake with upside-down progressive forks, a 23" front wheel (which no one was really doing yet), a stretched tank with no suspension in the back, which meant it looked killer but rode like a bucking horse. The shocks didn't shock with the angle of the tyre with the rake—it just bounced, and so did the hard rear end. I supermanned on it many times, which probably did not look cool now that I think of it, but it did turn heads, especially when one of the handlebars snapped off while riding out of my driveway on the second ride.

Because of the dodgy workmanship on the custom job (the handlebars broke twice), the club told me to put it in their shop and wouldn't let me ride it until they went over it, as I was now a Prospect in the outlaw motorcycle club.

On the day I was meant to pick it up, the motorbike shop that also joined the clubhouse burned down, and out of the 30-odd bikes, only mine and one other were insured. The funny part was that the other bike, which had been insured, had an identical paint job to mine—and I had designed mine to be original! So, back to the drawing board.

This time I was going to make the bike rideable. With the help of a few brothers and many, many hours of partying and many different transformations, it was rideable but still had a lot of bugs. So, I sent it to Gworks, which did an amazing job for the budget. Because it had been sitting for a while and had been through the ringer, we took the S&S motor out and put a stage 4 Screaming Eagle motor back in with a tyre shredder kit. However, this motor was faulty, so we went back to an S&S motor that I'm extremely happy with.

We have been through a lot together: countless toxic relationships, fires, clubs, crashes, injuries, friendships, losses, gains, extreme highs to extreme lows—and she's always been there for me, ready and eager to help make things right again. I will never sell this bike or replace her.

Now this bike has been in numerous photo shoots and newspaper articles that you will see later in this book, and has been a centre point in nearly every aspect of my life and countless others, which is why I think this story needs to be told. We used to have a saying: *It's not a lifestyle, it's a way of life—and those that don't understand it, never will!*

What was your experience in a 1% motorcycle club like? Were you only in the one club?

Just for some context, during my younger days, I bounced around a lot of different organisations such as the Army Cadets, the Country Fire Authority (CFA), various martial arts clubs, and groups that had an identity, like being a country boy or a horse rider in a western club. But instead of these always being something I *did*, they became a sense of identity for me, and I knew deep in the back of my brain that I was always going to be in a club. I started preparing myself for that, though it was all subconscious for me at the time, for the most part.

With that in mind, I co-founded and became president of one of the first Ute clubs in Australia pretty soon after getting my licence. There were about 30 of us—we had meetings, worked on each other's B&S Utes till all hours of the night, drinking and just being there for each other. We used to do everything together. Our group was inseparable. One of the members and I even bought a ute together that was a feral Ute show winner.

One month before my 21st birthday, my phone stopped ringing. No one would answer my calls, or if they did, they were staying home and not doing anything. I felt like I was basically being ghosted. Then, on the day of my 21st, I was wondering if anyone was even going to show up. I was sending out messages, starting to get a little panicked, when I heard this rumble come up the driveway. It was the ute of my dreams. All the members and their dads had been ghosting me because, for the last month, they had been working on this absolute basket case of a rusted-out ute I had bought with another member. They surprised me for my birthday.

It was done up the exact way I had told them I had wanted it. To me, this is what clubs were all about. They had been working on this thing night and day, with blood, sweat and tears, to make my dream become a reality—much like the outlaw motorcycle club members did for my motorbike when I wrote it off. This is one of my all-time favourite memories. Funny enough, two of these members ended up in the OMCG and other clubs I was part of.

I started flying over to and living in Thailand, doing Muay Thai kickboxing, which was unheard of back then. For a country boy, this was a very unusual thing to do. I was growing as a person and slowly drifted away, and that club disbanded. But I still craved being part of something.

Now I had bought a bike and was riding in some groups. This is where I met the first person in the chapters, giving us his story— Birol. We became close, and in a short period of time, we had a club called *The Wanderers Social Motorbike Club*, which I was a chapter president of, and my two mates from the Ute club came along for the ride as well. It was one of the first social clubs in Australia and is still running to this day.

This was a crazy amount of fun!

We got so well known at one point that some members of the "infamous Yandina 5," as quoted by Queensland's *Courier Mail*, actually wrote us a letter to try and help them get out of jail. They were put under the extreme VLAD laws, to which I was—and still am—very strongly opposed, as they take away people's basic human rights. There was a massive protest and we got to lead.

It wasn't uncommon for us to post a ride late Friday night and get 90 bikes show up on Saturday morning, which of course got the attention of some 1% clubs in the local area. It got me a pretty angry phone call from a club I didn't even know was still in the area at the time. Lucky for me, I had been around and had spoken to the other leading clubs in the area, and they vouched for my social club.

We had a fully decked-out shed on a farm, full of dirt bikes, a stage for bands, a target range, a bar, bedrooms and a kitchen on a lot of land. Our events were epic!

After a while, we linked up with four other social clubs. Out of those clubs, some of the wives and girlfriends even had their own motorcycle club, which had actually formed before the other social motorcycle clubs started gathering. It was just a coincidence, which happens a lot in the motorcycle community.

We all started going to heaps of rides together and co-hosting amazing events. However, another coincidence occurred—we all started associating with the same OMCG, but at different chapters across the state, as our clubs were located in different areas. Things were getting very tight—we were all almost like one club already, calling each other brothers and organising the same combined parties and events, until I got a call from the OMCG.

They told me they were expanding a worldwide back-patch motorcycle club that rode under them in other countries, and they were bringing it here. They wanted me to patch over my club and make me president, and offered us the world. For me, it fit—at the time, I was still travelling to Thailand often, and this club was actually one of the top clubs there. However, I loved my brothers, and I wouldn't step up and do this without them.

We had a meeting, and it was turned down, and I said no, I'm sticking with the Wanderers and my brothers. They said, No problem.

Over the next week or so, I put it behind me. But brothers were now calling me, asking more questions and showing signs they wanted it. We had another meeting, and it was essentially a 50/50 split down the middle. We decided to have another meeting with the OMCG and get some clarity on expectations and rules, but they sold it to us pretty hard. I spoke to the presidents of the other social clubs we were hanging around with at the time, and they also thought it seemed pretty cool as well.

Long story short, the OMCG got their new club and just about all of their chapters got to patch over chapters of the social clubs we were hanging around. Now we were all one club, which made sense since we did everything together anyway. We all knew each other well and had been riding together for two years non-stop. On top of that, we were now part of a worldwide club as one, and not five different clubs riding around as one.

Yes, as social club members, we still acted like a brotherhood with the other social motorcycle clubs, but it was just casual. Now we had the same colours—colours that people knew, colours that some people hated. This bonded us tightly and held people more accountable.

We ran with this hard and built up our club pretty strongly. We started behaving like 1%ers in some regards, only to be scolded by the OMCG members charged with supervising us. They said: if you want to act like 1%ers, you step up and do it right—or otherwise, knock it off.

Of course, being in this environment, the seeds were already planted, and everything we had been promised didn't come to fruition anyway. So, I called a sit-down with the president and asked about stepping up.

Another meaningful conversation I had was with a senior member whom I respected very much. I asked him, "Be honest—should I do it?" He said:

"You're already doing the job now, but without the patch. I can't answer this for you. But when you're 70 years old and telling your grandkids the story of your life, are you going to say, *I had the opportunity to be part of the biggest, baddest motorcycle club in the world and passed it up—or do you want to say, I was once a member of the biggest, baddest motorcycle club in the world and lived life to the max?"*

At this point, I knew what I was doing. The only question was—what was everyone else doing?

So, I called a meeting with the other members of my club. We all discussed it and thought, shit, we've come this far together. How much fun will it be if we all start the journey and go through it together? Talk about a bonding experience! At this point, we thought—why not?

Now the OMCG got a huge influx of prospects, and not only that—this group of prospects had already been riding together and working as a solid unit for years, and knew all the rules. It was a massive win for them and for us. If you thought we were tight before, it was nothing compared to how we were now. Everything we didn't like about the club, we knew that once we all got our patches, we could change it to be how we wanted, because we had huge numbers. It was a very exciting time.

After a while, I got offered a shorter prospect period because of my efforts and rank, but I declined, as this wasn't offered to all the men who followed me from one club to the next. It did get offered to a few of the people in the other chapters that started as presidents like I did—some took it and some didn't.

One thing clubs often pride themselves on is the time and effort it takes people to become a full member, and they often look down on people who choose the easy route, which it definitely did in this case. But I chose to stick with the men who had stuck with me, and do the whole time with them, because we were a team and had been through it all together. That's a story I wanted to continue and share that experience with them. And I'm so glad I did it that way.

From here, we all stepped up through the ranks together. I even did some of my prospecting time overseas with a few famous members, and got to lead a ride and party with one of my favourite Thai bands, which is one of the most famous bands in Thailand. I have a lot of standout memories from this time.

How did the experience shape who you are now?

You will get a sense of how the club changed me from some of the stories I tell, but it broke down a lot of my limiting beliefs and shattered a lot of cognitive biases I had.

The support I received allowed me the strength to work on myself because I knew I could rely on them, which eased my fear of abandonment.

Do you think your childhood or certain events in your upbringing led you to join a club?

During my younger days, I spent a lot of time with my uncle Colin. We listened to double-shot blues with George Thorogood blaring, and we would sing *I Drink Alone* and other cracking songs that I still love today.

There were always bikies coming around to his house when I was there. We would go to bikie parties with Maoris, having hāngis with all these tough kickboxers that I wanted to be like, as I always had a passion for martial arts. Plus, the respect and community they seemed to have for each other was always appealing— especially since I struggled to fit in as a kid.

Loyalty was a massive thing for my uncle. He talked about that and the importance of looking after family, which I have to say he has always followed through on—especially with the passing of my nan and pop, giving up everything to be their carer.

What do you think you got out of being in a motorcycle club that you were missing in your own life?

I address this topic extensively in other questions, but to summarise: **identity, meaning, and purpose.**

How did it benefit your life?

Personally, I had a series of traumatic events all happen close to one another, and the support I got from the brothers helped pull me through.

When I hurt my back really badly, they understood I couldn't ride and helped me with a lot of my personal duties—even cleaning my house and mowing my lawn. Some of the wives and girlfriends helped with the housework and cooked meals for me. When I ended up in hospital due to a hip reconstruction, which saw me in hospital for six weeks, they had a member with me at all times— just sitting there in case I woke up and needed anything.

Once I got out of the hospital, I was non-weight-bearing for the better part of a year, and members visited me daily when I was at home. At the time, I was living with a national (a high-ranking member) and his partner, and I will never forget what they did for me. A standout moment for me was having the most senior and most respected member anywhere help me put on my socks.

It may not sound like a big deal, but at the time I had gone from being the most highly independent guy to a defenceless, dependent man for the first time in my life—and I had the man I most respected, loved and looked up to, putting my socks on for me. Looking back, I guess I felt emasculated, but at the same time, I'll never forget the way he did it. I was shyly sitting in a chair, not wanting to ask, but I just couldn't get the job done. I said, "Really sorry, brother, can you please help me put my socks on?" He must have sensed my trepidation in asking and just went, "Of course, bro," like it was nothing, in a way that said, *You don't even need to ask, bro,* almost with a scoff of disbelief.

It's a moment burned into my brain. That was one of those life-changing moments—the moment of actually letting myself be helped and being forced to be vulnerable. It was most likely one of the first times I actually let someone in and hadn't been made to feel like I was a burden or an inconvenience. I will never forget that. It was a pivotal moment in my healing journey, and one I'm eternally grateful for.

The club always made sure I didn't miss out on anything. I always had members picking me up, running errands for me, and just being with me for months until I could drive again.

On top of my brother's passing and these life-changing injuries, which at the time they said I'd never ride my bike, lift over two kilograms, train martial arts or be able to work again, I also went through a very toxic and abusive relationship, which made me question my whole life. I used it as my conduit of change, and it became a defining moment. But at the time when I ended it, I was at my darkest point and didn't even want to leave the safety bubble of my house. With these things and a few others that had happened, I began to spiral and push everyone away. Everything happening together tore the bandage off the wound that had been cut when I was young, and it was all coming out at once. I was basically having a nervous breakdown.

I had a lot of anger that I had suppressed in my younger days, and it was all coming out now. And we always bleed on those that didn't cut us—it's always those we are closest to. It's a defence mechanism: *I'm going to push them away before they can hurt me.* And in some cases, we do it as a way to test if they really love us and we can trust them, because if they don't leave us, it means they do love us.

Oftentimes, this backfires and people leave—but not these brothers. They came to my house daily and tried to get me out. The Sergeant called me, as some of the brothers had told him I wasn't myself. Even my sister told me I was going to get locked up in the psych ward if I didn't calm down, as I had been doing some things way out of character and just hating the world, trying to start fights.

But I have to give them credit—the more I threatened them, the more they took the brunt of my storm. The Sergeant questioned me about it and I offered him out as well, all at once or one at a time. I said, and he said, "Brother, I'm just worried about you. What do I have to do to get you to talk to me? I'm not having a go at you, and it's staying with us. Come round and let's punch it out with me if that's what it takes, and then we can hug it out and have a beer afterwards."

I still remember this conversation, standing in the middle of the street near the Geelong hospital, as I had just gotten some bad news about my injuries. With the phone to my ear and tears streaming down my face, I was able to open up to him about my mental state—because he showed me he wasn't going anywhere and wasn't kicking me out or punishing me for acting out of character.

He was just there for me. This was another turning point in my healing. He actually asked me, "How can I help you, bro? How can I get through to you when you're off your fucking head?" And we put things in place that I agreed to, like a bit of leeway with attendance, some key phrases to snap me out of it, and that I had to keep them in the loop and be open with communication about where my head was at. Come to think of it, reflecting now, I was in a much worse space than I realised, and they went above and beyond for me. This is how a Sergeant should be!

Studies have shown that 80% of the healing benefit in therapy comes down to the relationship and trust levels—the other 20% is the work. Just having someone you trust to talk to can help immensely.

In fact, I remember seeing one of the older senior members cry for the first time in a room full of these vicious and terrifying men. You could have heard a pin drop as 30 members just listened to him with unconditional positive regard, followed by hugs and reassurance. This was a big step for someone who had been taught to suppress his emotions during childhood, because "real men don't cry," especially when they have to be the man of the house, which isn't actually in the job description for a child.

I later had a similar experience, and I got nothing but love from the brothers.

Having this support gave me the strength to continue my healing journey. However, this is not the case for the vast majority of people who join clubs, as many choose more alternative options that have very, very serious consequences. It definitely isn't all kittens and rainbows.

Unfortunately, you get a lot of people joining bike clubs for the wrong reasons. For those people, club life is usually very turbulent, to say the least.

How did it hinder your life?

When I started work as a trainee in the drug and alcohol field, I was still in the club. One of the people I was working with had been in jail for 23-odd years, and because of the VLAD laws (non-association laws), we couldn't be in the same room together or we would both be arrested—him because he was on parole, and me because I was in a criminal organisation. Obviously, this meant we were both "up to no good."

So, I decided it was hindering my life and my career. I had always said if it hindered my life in any way and did not add value to it, I'd leave. And with that, I made the nerve-wracking decision and asked to leave.

This phone call to my sponsor and long-time friend was one of the hardest things I've ever done, and I'm not ashamed to admit I cried during the call. Giving my hard-earned patches back was one of the hardest things I've had to do—but I was ready. I had outgrown the life.

I had meaning and purpose coming from other places. The partying, which I was famous for, had stopped a long time ago. I had gone from basically living at the clubhouse to barely being there, just scraping by on attendance. I had just been accepted into a degree in psychotherapy and had built a really good life for myself. I had started my own business, which I was struggling to keep up with. And a lot of the deeds that needed to be done as a member just seemed childish and ego-driven. I wasn't about to risk 15 years in jail because someone called us a name and lost everything I had worked for.

I was starting to date again, and these girls didn't care about the club or getting messed up. Instead, they wanted to talk about healing, trauma, growth, and goals.

This phone call, looking back, took me a year to make. I wanted to be absolutely sure. I didn't want to regret this choice—and it was such a huge thing for me. A part of who I thought I was. It was not a decision I made easily.

When I asked to leave, I'll never forget this word-for-word:

"Fuck, bro, we were wondering how you were going to live this life and do that work as well. What sort of brothers would we be to stand in the way of you bettering yourself and helping others?"

That made me even more upset. The very next day I was out on good standings.

Even though I was in good standing, I got unfollowed and deleted by hundreds of members worldwide overnight. The very next day, my phone went from being red-hot to dead quiet, in an instant. The silence was deafening. It was not uncommon for my phone to go flat twice a day, and on that day, I didn't even get a message or a phone call.

I talk about a lot of good things that happened to me while I was in a club, but I don't want to give you the wrong idea. I've had guns pulled on me by members of my own club because they were too fried and misunderstood the assignment. I was nearly set on fire and run over by a car with another brother. I've had "brothers" stab me in the back and hit on my partner at the time. I've been followed and harassed by the police. All of these things happened on numerous occasions.

I'm not going to go into all those stories, but you just need to know they happened—along with all the crazy in-fighting and drama in motorcycle clubs that could only be akin to that of a high school teenage girls' soap opera.

It's meant to be us against the world, but in most cases, it's us against us. For me, and for many others, that was the biggest disappointment of all.

Many men have been violently and falsely beaten out of clubs and put on bad standings because they found out another member was doing the wrong thing, but that member had the right friends up top. Or there was a disagreement, or someone lied or misperceived a situation while off their head and got some poor member in trouble when they didn't do anything.

You were constantly watching your back—like when a cop pulls up behind you at the lights, or when you walk through customs. Even though you haven't done anything wrong, you're still on edge,

24/7. But in a way, it's better than having to deal with your own emotional regulation problems.

Every time you got a message or a phone call, your first thought was: *For fuck's sake, what have I done now? Or for fuck's sake, what do they want now?*

But like in all abusive relationships, we say the highs are worth the lows—and in most cases, they aren't.

Do you have any standout stories or experiences you would like to tell and expand on?

Another thing that I think helped me in my healing journey was how you greet each other.

For me, during childhood and as a teenager, I was very uncomfortable in my own skin, and I hated being touched (unless it was from an intimate partner that I felt I could be vulnerable with). But when you do anything where there are brothers, you have to give them a handshake and a hug. A lot of brothers, especially with ethnic backgrounds, will also kiss you.

I remember my sponsor saying loudly on purpose for everyone to hear at one event—there were 30 brothers all greeting each other— he said: "Wow, there is a lot of man love going on right now."

This got a big laugh and cut the tension.

But for me, this was a massive invasion of my personal space. After a while, I realised this was okay. For a good old country boy who never touched other men, this went from being uncomfortable, to me lowering my guard and allowing that connection.

These brothers would also always say things like "Much love," "Much respect," and you hear something enough, you start to believe it—almost like an affirmation.

The brothers I still see now, we still do this.

Is there really a brotherhood or code/loyalty?

Absolutely, there is—but with individual members. You just need to find the real ones.

However, a lot of the loyalty is situational, and once the patch is gone or the circumstances don't suit some members, loyalty can be fleeting.

What would you say to people wishing to join a bike club for the first time?

Some advice for those looking to actually join a club: make sure they have a hard prospective and probationary period. The harder it is earned, the more people value it, and that club is likely to have better retention and brothers who respect their patch more.

On the same token, avoid new start-up clubs—including social motorcycle clubs. There are so many clubs out there, and if someone isn't joining one of those, it usually means:

1. They can't cut it and don't want to put in any effort—which is a red flag.

2. They probably just want to puff their chest out, call themselves a president or office bearer, and start a club so they can hold that title.

Later on, I talk about getting off the prohibited persons list. The friend who told me to follow it up and get myself off the list once gave up his dream job for me.

One day, he went for his dream job in customs. During the interview, they put up a picture of me and said, "He is a member of an OMCG on your friends list. We want you for this position, but you have to unfriend him and cease contact."

He told them to fuck off, as we had been mates since we were kids— and he lost the job.

With this in mind, it is very important to think about other people when joining a club and how it will affect those around you, because it will.

Another one of my childhood friends has an explosives licence, and he had to unfriend me. So did a mate's son who worked in a certain part of the army with a certain security level, which I always thought was odd, considering there were a lot of servicemen in the club.

You need to ask yourself: is it going to affect your ability to get a loan or have a business? Because they do have the power to squash that now and suspend your bank accounts—and yes, even if you haven't done anything wrong, it does happen.

Do you want your door kicked in, being ripped out of bed in front of your kids, even if you've done nothing wrong? This also happens to members.

How was your life initially after leaving a bike club, and how did you get out?

The void is real!

Like I said earlier, my phone used to go flat twice a day while I was in the club. The very next day after I left (even though I was on good standing), my phone was dead quiet—not a call, not a message. The silence was deafening. It opened me up to having to deal with all my issues, like tearing a Band-Aid off a bursting wound. This is the most common message I receive from members leaving a club: the void. It's why most of them go and join another one.

Dealing with this void can be tricky and different for everyone. When someone leaves a club, I always suggest seeing a psychologist first—you will be raw, and it's the perfect time to be doing something about it.

The second thing I suggest is volunteering. Find a foodbank, local community centre, or men's shed and give back to the community.

The third thing is exercise. The one thing all of us who have changed, healed, or been in recovery have in common is a daily fitness routine. So find a gym, or even better a sports team or martial arts club.

Fourth, you need to be doing something financial, like a job or something that will improve your position. It can even be saving $20 a week to start with.

And fifth, you should be doing something to improve your mental capacity—like learning an instrument, a language, learning about trauma, or studying one of the 1,000 free courses that are out there.

These little nuggets are actually from my *Five Keys to Happiness*, which covers mental, financial, physical, spiritual, and emotional connection.

Before you jump to conclusions, spirituality just means something bigger than yourself, like a motorcycle club that has church instead of meetings. We replace that with giving back.

All of these things combined are life-changing. Each one will have you out in the community, meeting people, doing good things, trying new things, expanding your mind, and giving you something else to talk about. It will also give you opportunities and networks.

We used to joke in the club that we had forgotten how to talk to "normal people" and that "normal people scared us." It's so easy to get wrapped up in that life that you forget how to navigate the real world. So you almost have to reintegrate as you would from prison.

These things keep you connected, making new healthy networks, finding new opportunities through putting yourself out there, while making your mind and body fit and strong, and learning new ways to cope.

From this, you will fall into something you love. You will find your meaning, purpose, and identity. It's easier said than done, yes—but definitely possible and very achievable.

Would you ever consider joining a club again?

Members always used to say, *"I've never met an ex-1%er that didn't want to be a 1%er again."* I always thought that was nonsense.

But if I'm being completely honest, there is a little part in nearly every ex-1%er I've spoken to that still misses elements of the club life, no matter how much therapy and void-filling they do. Myself included.

After a lot of soul-searching and after being asked many times if I still miss it after all these years, the answer is yes. You might be surprised to hear that, just as I'm surprised to be admitting it to myself. But this healing journey is a map without a destination. You just keep going over the territory and try to improve every day.

Years and years of romanticising, idealising, and participating in outlaw motorcycle club life cannot be forgotten in a short time— especially when my club time was actually pretty good. Sometimes I wonder, if I had had the bad experiences others had, would I think differently? But they don't seem to either—they still miss it too.

What's to miss? It's a great question—but I don't think it's the right one. *Why would you miss it now that your life is full?* That's a better question.

The healing game is not linear. People assume when you start healing that it's onwards and upwards, which couldn't be further from the truth. I've mentioned before that the club is becoming a source of identity, meaning, and purpose. I also mentioned that if you don't have good coping skills and want to avoid accountability and responsibility, it's a pretty good place to shift your focus and concentrate all your energy on trivial drama.

This is a roundabout way of saying—with all the stresses of life, some people want to take a holiday overseas to escape, some put their head in a book, smash a crazy weight session, get high on drugs... or romanticise about being in a motorcycle club.

I once heard this joke, and I think there is some truth to it; I said to my mum, *"When I grow up, I want to be a bikie."* She replied, *"I'm sorry, son, you can't do both."*

Now, in my life, I have huge responsibilities and a lot of people counting on me. It can be stressful. We all have good and bad days, no matter how much you think you've grown. If you're following a guru who says life is always amazing, he's a con man. Life is great— but it can also be hard, and harder if you are healing and your default setting says: *I'm stressed because of all the responsibility I have—but hang on, I know a place that was just sex, drugs and rock and roll with no responsibility.*

Then we trigger cognitive dissonance, which blocks out the bad stuff and only remembers the fun parts of club life. That romanticised fantasy creeps back in.

When this happens, I acknowledge the train of thought, put it on the cloud that looks like a motorcycle inside my head, and watch it float away—remembering how good a life I have now. I'm grateful for my time in the club, because I wouldn't be in the position I am now without it.

A hard part for me personally is that I'd rather not talk about outlaw motorcycle clubs at all. But unfortunately, if all I did was talk about trauma, I wouldn't engage the people I'm trying to reach. Always talking about club life keeps a slight hold on me.

For example, you might be reading this book for the bikie stuff, but now you know words like trauma, cognitive dissonance, identity, and meaning. I've slipped a heap of these into this "bikie book." But if you ask me, this is really a book on trauma and mental health. It's made you self-reflect and improved your mental health vocabulary—planting seeds, joining dots, helping you discover why you do the things you do. And you didn't even know you were reading a workbook.

I digress. For the context of this question, I'd never join another 1% club.

How is your life now after some time away from club life?

Honestly, like many other brothers, I thought I'd never ride again without that patch on my back. I thought I'd feel naked. But that passed in the first ten minutes of riding without it.

The first set of traffic lights I pulled up to, I split the traffic, rode to the front, and sat there tapping my feet to the music in my head (which, when I'm riding, has always been only three different songs). For the first time, I wasn't paranoid about anyone coming and knocking me off my bike, which has happened to numerous members in my time.

On that same ride, I pulled up beside a cop car, and they left me alone for the first time in a long time. I had just got the new engine in the Harley, so I thought I'd take her for a run and give it a bit to wear it in correctly. I was hooking down a country back road when a cop came the other way. Lights and sirens came on, and he pulled up behind me.

After I stopped, the first thing he said was, *"Thanks for stopping."* We had a little laugh, and he asked why I was going at a ludicrous speed. I explained the new engine and the need to run it in. He took my licence and checked it. I know from experience that this never wins me any favours, and I've lost my licence a few times. It never bothered me before, because I'd just fly back to Thailand for the duration. But this time, he came back, gave me my licence, and said, *"Watch the speed. Have a good day."*

He drove away, and I was left sitting there wondering if I should even ride off. This was new to me—not being half strip-searched on the side of the road. I waited for the fine to come, but it never did.

That, and the phone not going off its head, were two completely new experiences.

My partner and I were travelling once and got stopped and searched at the airport. They confiscated our phones and went through absolutely everything we had. While this was normal for me, it wasn't a life my partner was used to. I knew eventually something would have to be done about it, as we planned to do a lot more travelling.

Once you join a motorcycle club, if you have a firearms licence, it gets taken off you, along with your firearms. During my younger years, I had planned to get my firearms licence. I actually did the test three times and passed, but never handed in the paperwork.

Now that I'm on a healing journey, I thought I'd start ticking off all the boxes I'd left unchecked. I did the test, handed it in, and guess what? I was listed as a prohibited person due to being a member of a club. No dice. But there was a link to contest it, which one of my good friends pushed me to follow through with; otherwise, it would follow me for life.

By now, I'd been working in the mental health industry for a while. I got 15 different references from good-standing people in the community, sent all the links for my social media, my new qualifications, and a statutory declaration saying I was a changed man and no longer in the club. A week later, my licence showed up in the mail.

Holy shit—the system works! This was mind-blowing to me. Looking back, I can understand why they didn't think I should have a firearm. Even a senior member once told me: *"If you have a gun, keep it an hour away from your house. That way if you ever get angry, you have at least two hours to calm down before making a silly choice."* Even he knew it wasn't a good idea. But now my perception of what I had believed to be true was being stripped away.

Since then, I've been through 27 different countries and never been searched once.

I travelled to those 27 countries to train in each country's original martial art—something I thought was never going to happen with my injuries. On top of that, I ticked off a bucket list of crazy activities: skiing in New Zealand, extreme 4x4 in the sand dunes of Abu Dhabi, getting engaged on top of a volcano in Indonesia, white-water rafting in France, seeing must-see attractions around the world, and some hidden gems like being in a carnival in the bottom of a salt mine in Romania before visiting Count Dracula's castle.

I also visited some of the world's most historic sites in the UK and Poland, as well as the birthplaces of both sides of my family tree in the Netherlands and Wales.

I've always wanted to live permanently in Thailand. Now I'm at a stage in my life where I can if I want to. We actually own a farm in my wife's country town. But I'm so content with crushing life here in Australia that I'll just travel back and forth—which is fantastic.

I got married on the beach at sunset in Thailand, with all my family present, to the most beautifully hearted and mentally healthy woman. She supports me through everything, is very understanding of how much time my endeavours keep me busy, and puts up with me having a new idea every ten minutes. Being the best cook in the world doesn't hurt either!

My friends are the coolest people I've ever met. We constantly talk about wins, goals, and dreams—checking in on each other daily. I still get to ride around with many of the identical boys I used to, but now we do it for good causes.

This book, I'm creating a documentary, and I realise that my social media, non-profit, business, and personal life would not be where they are today without all the experiences that have shaped me. For that, I am incredibly grateful.

If you had your time over again, would you still do it?

The reality is—I wouldn't be where I am today without it. So yes.

If I didn't do it, I'd always wonder what it was like, and probably end up being one of those sad middle-aged men who live in regret and keep talking about the good old days, trying to get my kids to follow my dream.

Even my mum said, *"I'm glad you got it out of your system."*

That doesn't mean I'd recommend it to anyone else, though.

If you had children and they wanted to join a club, what would you say to them?

I would be completely honest and tell them my experiences—the good, the bad, and the ugly.

But I would also tell them that I've had some of the most unforgettable experiences of my life because of the club, and I met some of the best people I've ever known. I'd also tell them about the betrayals, the politics, and the constant fear of police harassment, jail, or even death.

At the end of the day, I'd support them no matter what—but I'd make sure they fully understood what they were walking into.

Have you had any Mental Health issues, and did you get treatment?

After all my life-altering experiences, Workcover sent me to see a psychiatrist, and I got diagnosed with Complex Trauma, Adjustment Disorder with Depressed mood and Anxiety, which led me to see a psychologist. One thing I do find interesting is the number of bikies and ex-bikes like myself and others in this book that have ADHD is huge; someone needs to look into that.

Thanks to the help of a really good General Practitioner GP, I was also seeing a good physiotherapist and a great Psychologist for my rehabilitation.

Over time, I began training and doing all my rehab both inside and outside the gym, and I started fixing a body that was said to be unfixable. I was seeing the psychologist at least once a week for three years, and then every other week and then every six weeks for another three years.

During my healing journey, I experienced intense anxiety and often couldn't bring myself to leave the house. I went through deep catharsis, weeks where I couldn't stop crying and was completely overwhelmed by emotion. My body was flooded with stress chemicals, and for months, I rarely slept more than an hour a night. In my search for understanding, I threw myself into study, sometimes for up to 23 hours a day, and became what I now call a trauma nerd. At first, I was driven by a need for closure, wanting to understand why someone who claimed to love me could treat me so poorly. But soon my focus shifted inward, to understand why I allowed it, how my own patterns and actions had led me to that point, and how I could finally break the cycle and stop reliving the same pain.

Then once I finished my counselling qualifications, I got asked if I wanted to do a Traineeship in Alcohol and Other Drugs. I jumped at the chance, and in our first meeting with all the other trainees, the employer started talking about pay rates, and I put up my hand and asked, "Do we get paid for this? Everyone laughed and said yes, I had no idea, I was just happy to be learning, helping and using my new skills as a counsellor.

Do you still see anyone from your days in the bike club?

Members and ex-members reach out to me on a weekly and sometimes daily basis, some struggling with their mental health, especially if they have left, and some just want to touch base for a chat. Nearly all those members I spoke about earlier, and nearly all the members I was in the club with, are now out, and the majority of them have been in touch with me for some advice or to catch up for a ride.

Every now and again, someone will leave and add me on social media, and that's cool. I also deleted members I was friends with who were removed due to non-association while I was in the club; it's just how it is; it's not personal.

I get messages from current members in clubs, so if you're wondering if I have gotten any heat from my social media or for even announcing I'm doing a book, no I haven't; in fact, feedback from clubs has been positive, really positive!

Some people aren't happy with me doing this and call me a snitch or whatever. Still, I just say to them, I'll be here for you to call on when you eventually need it. I'm not talking about anything you can't find on Google, plus for the most part, I'm thinking I'm helping change the narrative and put elements of them in a better light. I'm one of the only people out here saying there are good parts to it; it's factual to my experience. I try to be as non-biased as possible. I'm not writing this book full of lies, trying to claim how cool I was; my intention is to help, and if it helps some of their members, former members, or the general public, why would they hate it?

Respect is the key in the motorcycle world, and I was already doing social media before I left the club. They asked one thing of me: "We love what you're doing, bro, but please don't mention the club's name", so I don't.

The other reason I don't mention the club name is because of alienation. I'm collaborating with a heap of men in this book, and for the first few weeks, I didn't even know what clubs they were from; it doesn't matter, if it weren't for a patch, we would all be best mates.

Now imagine that all of us had of been blasting what club we were from all over the place, it may have stopped us reaching out to one another because of past grievances, or it could have stopped one of these current members from other clubs reaching out to me for help, because of what my colours used to be, it doesn't bloody matter.

Plus, you will also see a lot of these men talk about how the club changed. One particular comment said that they "joined a club, and left a gang" I have heard many people say this, so just because I was in a club back then, it may have changed, and something I say may not be true anymore.

Do you still ride now, and what do you ride?
Yes—I'll never stop riding.

I still have my Harley Softail, the same one that has been rebuilt and customised so many times over the years. She's been through fires, crashes, rebuilds, and countless memories.

I'll never sell her. She's part of me, and part of my story.

What did you learn about yourself through your time in and out of the club?

That I'm stronger than I ever gave myself credit for.

I learned that loyalty, love, and brotherhood are possible, but they're not guaranteed just because someone wears the same patch.

I learned that I can survive loss, pain, betrayal, heartbreak and still find purpose, healing, and joy.

Most importantly, I learned that my past doesn't define me. It shaped me, but it doesn't own me.

What message would you give to people reading this book?

That no matter where you've been or what you've done, change is possible.

You can take the lessons from your past, the good and the bad and use them to build something better.

Don't let shame or fear hold you back. Your story isn't over, and you have the power to write the next chapter.

Is there anything else you'd like to add?

I'd like to address a misconception and crime in motorcycle clubs, painting all bikies with the same brush because a few, means you can say the same of the police force and all their convictions in the past. Just because one football player gets caught selling or doing drugs doesn't mean the whole football club does, and it's ludicrous to assume that bike clubs are any different.

I was in one of the top 4 outlaw motorcycle clubs in the world, and the majority of its members all had full-time jobs and a family. I'm not saying crime doesn't happen like it does everywhere, but what I'm saying is that in most clubs, it's not organised crime at all. We used to constantly say we couldn't organise a party half the time, let alone organise crime. A quote I heard once was "clubs are not criminal organisations, they just have some criminals in them", which is true!

Just that life is short, and it's too precious to waste living someone else's dream or trapped in someone else's version of loyalty.

I'm grateful for my time in the club because it gave me stories, lessons, and strength - but I'm even more grateful for the life I've built since leaving.

If you're struggling, reach out. If you're lost, keep searching. And if you think you can't change, you're wrong. You can.

CHAPTER NINETEEN

TROY'S BLURB

People often assume that being an ex-bikie would be a barrier to building a career in mental health and community support. But for me, it's been the opposite. That lived experience has become one of my greatest assets. It's what allows me to reach people who wouldn't normally ask for help. When someone looks at me and says, "What the hell would you know about changing your life? Books don't teach that," I can say, "What if I read those same books... but also lived the life you're living?" That's when the bravado drops. That's when they lean in and say, "Alright, bro. What do I have to do?"

I'm now the Founder and CEO of Complete Health Geelong CHG, which is fast becoming an industry leader that's redefining how we support people through Mental Health, Disability, and Addiction.

What started as a vision rooted in lived experience has become an industry leader, one that's trauma-informed, community-driven, and with a no trigger warning approach.

WHAT WE DO

Complete Health Geelong is more than a service provider—it's a movement. We've built a powerhouse team of Support Workers,

Counsellors, and Personal Trainers who deliver over 11-day programs and seven free community gym sessions every week. Every session is backed by qualified counsellors and designed to meet people where they're at—no judgment, no bullshit.

We run courses on Overcoming Complex Trauma and Co-Dependency to change those patterns of behaviour, aiming for long-lasting behavioural change. This approach believes that to change the fruit, we need to change the roots of the tree. We have also launched a Motorbike Building Program for disengaged youth.

One of our most transformative offerings is Exercise Psychotherapy. This isn't just about fitness—it's about rewiring behaviour through movement. We work with people facing addiction, personality disorders, depression, anxiety, and relationship challenges. Through Weight Training, Circuit Training, and mixed martial arts, we help individuals build boundaries, reclaim their identity, and rediscover meaning. Every course is infused with Yoga, guided meditation, and gratitude practices, so mindfulness becomes second nature—often without people even realising it.

THE FREE COMMUNITY GYM

Mental health and physical health are closely intertwined. That's why we created our Free Community Gym—a space where support is accessible, stigma is shattered, and healing happens through connection.

These aren't just workouts. Each session includes psychoeducation, mindfulness, and gratitude practices to support emotional regulation and wellbeing. A Qualified Counsellor and Personal Trainer lead every group. We've built rituals into the week that foster community: High Tea for the Ladies Group on Mondays, and a BBQ for the Men's Group on Fridays.

We use a two-pronged therapeutic approach:

1. Top-down therapy is talking, but this can be hard for some people and can bring on all sorts of somatic experiences, releasing toxic chemicals in the body. But talking is how we can process hard topics.

2. Also work from a bottom-up approach, which helps people connect with their bodies, burn off bad chemicals while releasing endorphins that make you feel good, but also gives you something else to focus on, so it's easier to talk about.

This integration of mind and body is what makes our programs so effective—and so different.

The gym is open to everyone, and every session is free—because we believe support shouldn't come with a price tag, and we got sick of not being able to offer people help then and there, because if you turned them away, you would never see them again, which brings us to our Sponsorships that bridge the gaps.

At CHG, we know that financial hardship shouldn't be a barrier to healing. That's why we've built a robust sponsorship model to ensure no one falls through the cracks.

We offer:

1. Individual Sponsorships – Covering costs for counselling, gym, and support services

2. Event Sponsorships – Funding community events or hosting free BBQs with mental health teams present

3. Barrier-Free Access – Paying out-of-pocket expenses for support services not covered by NDIS, especially for youth with disabilities

These sponsorships are funded and administered directly by Complete Health Geelong, with support from aligned organisations, such as The Mental Health Militia.

I'm also the Founder and one of the Directors of The Mental Health Militia, a not-for-profit organisation that supports CHG's mission with boots-on-the-ground support. While it may look like a motorcycle club, it's actually a network of lived-experience professionals—counsellors, psychologists, nurses, and advocates—who ride, volunteer, and amplify CHG's reach.

The Militia helps deliver CHG's community BBQs, supports events, and contributes volunteer hours. It's a symbol of what's possible when people from all walks of life come together to serve a common cause.

OUR IMPACT

In 2024, Complete Health Geelong, with support from The Mental Health Militia, delivered:

- Over 15,000 hours of direct support

- 1,200+ volunteer hours

- 1,600+ meals served at Mental Health BBQs

- Thousands of hours of free support for those who couldn't afford it

- 9 community organisations and events sponsored

- 12 charity events attended, with three keynote talks given

- 600+ gifts donated

- 70+ individuals sponsored for out-of-pocket support

- International outreach, including sponsorship of an orphanage and an underprivileged school in Thailand

WHY IT MATTERS

Complete Health Geelong isn't just a service provider—it's a blueprint for what happens when lived experience meets professional excellence. It's proof that healing doesn't have to look clinical. That support can come from someone who's walked through fire and lived to tell the story. That transformation is possible—and contagious.

This chapter isn't just about what we've built. It's about what's possible when you stop trying to fit into the system and start building your own.

At CHG, our mission doesn't stop at the gym door or the counselling room; it extends into the digital world, where we offer free advice, lived experience insights, and real-time connection to thousands of people who might never walk into a clinic.

Every week, I go live on social media with The Knockaround Guys—a crew of lived experience advocates who've walked the hard roads and come out the other side. We call it Lived Experience Yarns, and it's raw, honest, and deeply human. I'm joined by legends like Jacob Little from About Time for Justice, and Dennis from Run That Rehab—two men who've turned their own battles into platforms for change.

These Monday night lives aren't just content—they're community. We talk about trauma, addiction, recovery, relationships, identity, and everything in between. No scripts. No filters. Just real talk from real people who've lived it. And every week, someone new reaches out and says, "I saw your live… I think I'm ready to get help."

SOCIAL MEDIA AS A LIFELINE

Across our social platforms, CHG offers free advice, mental health education, and daily motivation. We break down complex topics into accessible language, share tools for emotional regulation, and spotlight stories of transformation. It's not about going viral—it's about going vital. Reaching the people who need it most, in the moments they're most likely to listen.

We use reels, posts, lives, and podcasts to make healing visible—and to show that support doesn't have to be clinical or complicated. Sometimes, it's just a comment, a DM, or a shared story that opens the door.

THE ANNUAL MEN'S MENTAL HEALTH EVENT

One of our proudest achievements is the Massive Men's Mental Health Family Fun Day event that we run every year. We have 10 inspiring Guest speakers, a Car, a Bike, and a Ute show, all designed to break the stigma and build brotherhood, showing that if guys like us can change, you can too.

This event is a celebration of vulnerability, strength, and shared experience. There are bands all day, food trucks, free mental health support, service providers, market stalls and carnival rides.

Unfortunately, my skills rest there, and that means we do not receive any funding for anything we do. I self-fund these programs for the most part, which brings us back to the social media, the merchandise, the event and this book. These things are all so I can keep funding these free community programs and try to expand them across Australia. These programs work, and I don't have the knowledge or the time to get them where they need to be. If things like this book can help me keep these programs alive, I'll do it.

If you would like to donate, sponsor or volunteer your services to help me make this dream a reality, I would love to hear from you. We will also be looking for more people to interview for the next installment of this series.

I will add that, since changing my life, I have had the pleasure of working with some international people that I could only have dreamed of meeting. I've literally met all my heroes in this space. Don't think that because you have a past, you can't do things; if anything, it makes you better for this space.

Don't be a cowboy, get qualified, stay evidence-based!

TRAUMA AND ITS EFFECTS

You've now read the stories of men and women who have walked the hard road of club life. I spoke of brotherhood that turned to paranoia. Gerry shared the weight of loyalty and the cost it demanded. Jacob remembered the pull of belonging and the price he paid for it. Others told of violence, addiction, broken families, and the search for identity that stitched them into the fabric of the club.

What connects all of these stories is not just the patch on their back, but the pain carried underneath. Childhoods marked by neglect, homes scarred by violence, relationships strained by betrayal, and the constant struggle of trying to feel "enough."

This is the thread running through every voice — trauma. It's the force that shapes behaviour, choices, and even the need for the brotherhood and sisterhood these men and women found. Some tried to bury it, some wore it like armour, and others only faced it once they walked away.

That's where we turn now. To understand these lives, we need to understand trauma — what it is, how it works, and how it explains so much of what you've just read.

First things first, what is trauma and how does it affect us? You probably have a good idea of what trauma is, but you might not know that there are other types of trauma. Meet Kaiser and his study of Adverse Childhood Experiences, otherwise known as Complex Trauma.

The study into Adverse Childhood Experiences is the world's largest study of its kind, with over 800,000 people to date. The original study involved 17,000!

Trauma is now defined as any event that has a long-lasting constant negative emotion, and the event only needs to be perceived as that — not necessarily factual. What is traumatic to a 3-year-old is totally different to what's traumatic to a 30-year-old, but traumatic nonetheless.

What Kaiser found was that a one-off traumatic experience and lots of small traumatic experiences actually create the same chemical reaction in the body. Think about it this way: both are out of your control, both are scary, both leave you waiting for a lion to jump out and get you, and both leave long-lasting negative emotions.

Another way to think of this is: let's say as a child a caregiver consistently made you feel bad about yourself. For example:

1. You tried to tie your shoelaces and it took too many attempts. This was met with eye-rolling and frustration, making you feel stupid.

2. You tried to help do the dishes — above the pay grade for your age — and you messed it up, only to be told: *"Bloody hell, here, let me do it. If you can't do it right, don't do it at all,"* making you feel less than.

3. You were playing with your toys only to be told *"Kids are meant to be seen and not heard,"* teaching you that you're not important and that authority figures are the fun police and not to be listened to.

4. You simply asked for something, trying to get a need met, and instead of having the situation explained, you got a lecture about how ungrateful you are because *"we do everything for you."* This taught you that you're a burden, when in fact it was their choice to have you — they actually owe you everything, not the other way around.

5. You got told *"You're the man of the house, it's time you acted like it,"* which was parentification — giving you a responsibility you couldn't live up to. This taught you your worth was only that of being "the man of the house."

6. You got triangulated and pitted against your siblings with things like *"Why can't you be like your brother/sister?"* This often created a need for justice because you always got punished harshly, over-criticised, and judged unfairly compared to everyone else.

7. You got broken promises all the time. For example: on Monday you were told you'd be going somewhere amazing on Saturday. After waiting all week in excitement, Saturday came and you were told you couldn't go because something "came up." This taught you that if you have to wait for something, it probably won't happen — making you impatient.

8. You had to keep secrets and constantly got told *"Blood is thicker than water"* and *"Family is everything,"* teaching you blind loyalty. This makes you stay in toxic situations longer than you should, at your own detriment.

9. You had no safe space of your own. People would enter your room even when you said no, read your private journal, or

break your favourite toy — teaching you not to have boundaries.

10. You had to look and behave one way outside the house and differently at home. This taught you that what others think on the outside is more important than what's on the inside, creating a need for external validation.

11. You were told *"Real men don't cry"* — when they do. Crying is natural and relieves stress. Instead, you bottled it up like a Coke bottle rolling down stairs, ready to explode in rage.

12. You only ever got praised when doing something for your caregiver. This taught you that your worth only comes when you do things for others, turning you into a "nice guy" or a people-pleaser.

13. You constantly got shut down for showing emotions because your caregivers also didn't know how to regulate theirs. You stopped feeling and processing emotions, becoming an overthinker — but you can't outthink a feeling problem.

14. Because everything was always only "good" or "bad," you learnt to see the world in black and white. In reality, life is full of colour. This caused heaps of relationship problems.

15. You witnessed toxic relationships and were gaslit: being told *"Come here, we won't hurt you,"* only to be slapped and then told *"Sorry, I love you."* This taught you that relationships are meant to be painful.

16. You learnt that if the car pulled up the driveway too fast or the door slammed too hard, it meant your caregiver was angry — and you were in for a rough night. You became like a sonar, always scanning for danger, back to the wall, reading everyone in the room.

While these things may sound trivial, when consistent they leave long-lasting negative emotions. The body releases stress chemicals that cause inflammation and autoimmune problems later in life.

It also affects a child's development. To a child, an adult is like a god — they know everything, they control survival. If they're never wrong, then the child must be wrong. If they constantly make you feel worthless, stupid, or bad, you internalise it: *"I'm stupid, I'm bad, I'm worthless, I'm not enough."* This belief is at the root of many mental health issues.

Instead of thinking *"I did a bad job washing because I'm a kid, it was my first time, and I'm still learning,"* you learn *"I'm a piece of shit who can't get anything right."* That's the difference between guilt and shame. Guilt says *"I did something wrong, but I can fix it."* Shame says *"I am wrong — I'm no good."*

If a child can't escape (fight or flight), they turn inward. They block out their feelings to survive. Self-reflecting when all you feel is pain is too much. So you disconnect from yourself, and when you can't connect with yourself, you can't connect with others either — because that could mean more pain. It leaves you feeling alone in a room full of people.

Children in these situations often struggle at school or in activities. They may seek attention in the wrong places, or lose themselves in books, music, or sports — because it's hard to focus on "351 × 253 = ?" when you're worrying about what you'll walk into at home. Sometimes it's easier to be invisible, to escape into imagination. But while you're worrying about survival, you're not finding out who you are. You don't discover your passions, your identity. Instead, you grow up trying to fill a void — with people, drugs, sports, food, risk-taking. Nothing fills it, because it's like a bucket with a hole in it.

Most of the men in this book would score in the high or very high range on the ACEs test. If you'd like to know your own score, please google the test. (If you hesitate on a question, the answer is "yes".)

If you score 4 or more, it's wise to get a health check. Also, see a psychologist or counsellor — even for a chat — to make sure you're okay. It's also a good idea to try yoga or a martial art with meditation, and regular exercise to burn off stress chemicals.

Just knowing about ACEs can be life-changing. Awareness can break the cycle for the next generation. It's not all doom and gloom. Think of this as a tool to find a starting point for healing. You can say: *"Wow, all this time I thought there was something wrong with me, but actually, things just happened to me. Little me didn't know how to handle it — and I'm not alone."*

The good news: what is learnt can be unlearnt. You're not broken — you're just over-adapted!

MORPHEUS PUBLISHING

EXPRESSION OF INTEREST

Our Anthology of Men's Stories for Men's Mental Health

Have you ever wanted to write your own story?

Maybe there's something inside you that's been waiting to be told — a life lesson, a challenge, or a moment that changed everything. Perhaps you've thought about putting it into words, but weren't sure where to start.

Now is your chance.

We're inviting men from all walks of life to contribute to *Our Anthology of Men's Stories for Men's Mental Health* — a raw and powerful collection of real experiences told by real men. This project is about courage, healing, and connection. It's about breaking the silence, dismantling stigma, and reminding others that they are not alone.

Your story doesn't have to be perfect. It just has to be honest. Every voice adds strength to the message that it's okay to talk, it's OK to feel, and it's OK to heal.

A portion of the book's profits will go to **Mental Health Militia,** supporting their work in men's wellbeing and suicide prevention. By sharing your story, you'll not only be helping yourself but also helping others find hope through your words.

If you've ever wanted to make a difference, now's the time to put pen to paper.

To express your interest in contributing to this anthology — or if you have a full book idea that aligns with men's mental health, resilience, or lived experience — submit your proposal through **Morpheus Publishing**.

PUBLISHING WITH MORPHEUS PUBLISHING

Morpheus Publishing is an Australian independent publisher dedicated to helping real people share real stories. We guide writers through every stage of the publishing journey — from writing and editing to design, production, and promotion — ensuring your story reaches readers in a professional, powerful way.

Whether you're writing a chapter for this anthology or have a complete manuscript ready to go, Morpheus Publishing offers supportive, accessible pathways to bring your story to life.

JOIN OUR WRITING GROUP

If you're not sure where to start, our **Morpheus Writing Group** is the perfect place to begin. This supportive, community-based group helps you develop your writing, build confidence, and connect with other storytellers who are also on the journey of sharing their truth.

You'll receive guidance on structure, storytelling, and self-expression — all in a safe space that encourages growth, connection, and creativity. Many of our published authors started right here, learning the craft and finding their voice before becoming part of an anthology or publishing their own book.

Your story matters.

Whether it's a chapter, a memoir, or a message the world needs to hear, Morpheus Publishing is here to help you tell it.

www.morpheuspublishing.com.au

hello@morpheuspublishing.com.au

MENTAL HEALTH MILITIA FOUNDATION
CONTACT DETAILS

If you or someone you know needs help please contact
Mental Health Militia Foundation

Website: https://www.mentalhealthmilitia.org.au/
Email: contact@mentalhealthmilitia.org.au

QR CODE MENTAL HEALTH